Glaus

Mina

Dorssen

Van   Leticia   Iris

CONTENTS

Accomplishments of the Duke's Daughter

3

WRITTEN BY

Reia

ILLUSTRATED BY

Haduki Futaba

Airship

Seven Seas Entertainment

BERNE DARSHI ARMELIA
Son of Duke Armelia.
Had feelings for Yuri.

GLAUS
Boss of the Boltik family, which
controls east Armelia.

RUDIUS GIB ANDERSON
Childhood friend of and
advisor to Prince Alfred.

DORSSEN KATABERIA
Son of the knight commander.
Has a crush on Yuri.

VAN LUTASHA
Son of the pope of the Darryl
Church. In love with Yuri.

YURI NEUER
Daughter of Baron Neuer. Built a
reverse harem at the academy.

characters

ACCOMPLISHMENTS OF THE DUKE'S DAUGHTER CAST OF CHARACTERS

EDWARD TONE TASMERIA
Second prince of Tasmeria.
Formerly engaged to Iris.

ELLIA
The current queen.
Edward's mother.

SHARIA
First wife of the current
king, mother to Alfred
and Leticia. Deceased.

IRIA FONS TASMERIA
The queen dowager. Retired
from public life and resides
in the detached palace.

GAZELL DAZ ANDERSON
Marquis Anderson and general
of Tasmeria. Merellis's father.

LOUIS DE ARMELIA
Duke of Armelia and
the prime minister of
Tasmeria. Iris's father.

DIDA

Iris's bodyguard. She took him
in when he was a child.

LYLE

Iris's bodyguard. She took him
in when he was a child.

IRIS LANA ARMELIA

Daughter of the Duke of Armelia.
Regained memories from a past life.

REHME

House Armelia's librarian. Iris took
her in when she was a child.

TANYA

Iris's handmaid. She took her
in when she was a child.

DEAN

Temporary employee of the Azuta
Corporation. Very skilled.

MERELLIS REISER ARMELIA

Wife of Duke Armelia and the Flower
of High Society. Iris's mother.

MINA

Takes care of the children at
the church Iris supports.

LETICIA

Dean's younger sister. Very
intelligent, has a knack for politics.

KOUSHAKU REIJOU NO TASHINAMI Vol.3
©Reia, Haduki Futaba 2016
First published in Japan in 2016 by
KADOKAWA CORPORATION, Tokyo.
English translation rights arranged with
KADOKAWA CORPORATION, Tokyo.

Seven Seas press and purchase enquiries can be sent to
Marketing Manager Lianne Sentar at press@gomanga.com.
Information regarding the distribution and purchase of
digital editions is available from Digital Manager CK Russell
at digital@gomanga.com.

Follow Seven Seas Entertainment online at
sevenseasentertainment.com.

TRANSLATION: Andria Cheng
COVER DESIGN: Hanase Qi
INTERIOR LAYOUT & DESIGN: Clay Gardner
PROOFREADER: Meg van Huygen, Jade Gardner
LIGHT NOVEL EDITOR: E.M. Candon
PREPRESS TECHNICIAN: Rhiannon Rasmussen-Silverstein
PRODUCTION MANAGER: Lissa Pattillo
MANAGING EDITOR: Julie Davis
ASSOCIATE PUBLISHER: Adam Arnold
PUBLISHER: Jason DeAngelis

ISBN: 978-1-64827-456-5
Printed in Canada
First Printing: November 2021
10 9 8 7 6 5 4 3 2 1

CHAPTER 11

The Duke's Daughter, Talk of the Town

PRINCESS LETICIA, known to her intimates as Letty, entered the room with a sigh. As the blood sister of Prince Alfred, she was third in line for the throne. A beautiful girl with blonde hair and soft green eyes the color of peridots, Letty bore a striking resemblance to her late mother, Queen Sharia—though to be honest, Alfred remembered the queen only faintly. Now his sister's lovely features had sharpened with concern.

"Brother, I can't take you to task if you've already made your move, but wouldn't it have been wiser to use your brain first?"

"Letty, have you finished?"

"I have. And all while you were busy with your scheming and meeting with your little sweetheart." A charming smile was plastered on her face, but her eyes held no hint of that expression. She took a step forward and silently placed the documents she was holding on the desk. "This one's free of charge. I noticed something suspicious about our financial flow."

Leticia had taken care of Alfred's business while he was away. His work had continued to pile up since the king's illness, and he wouldn't have been able to tear himself away from his desk if not for his sister's help.

Sadly, even as a child, Leticia had been all too aware of her precarious situation within the palace—that is, that she was right in the center of a power struggle. Yet not only had she received a formal education, she had learned how to conduct all the family business as well. Even Duke Armelia, the prime minister himself, had recognized her political acumen and analytical skill.

"You've grown even more efficient at this, Letty. I feel secure knowing I can continue entrusting the work to you."

"Hmm, I hope you're not already planning your next trip, Brother?"

Alfred flipped through the report as he listened to Leticia. He couldn't think of one thing he would add to it. In fact, she had covered the matter so exhaustively that the report included elements Alfred himself wouldn't have thought to address.

"The Minister of Human Affairs has chosen to side with the second prince. As such, he's pushed less consequential projects like this one to the side."

"So it goes..."

The capital's seven governing bodies ran the kingdom: the Ministries of Finance, Defense, Law, Foreign Affairs, Infrastructure, Human Affairs, and Education. The prime minister oversaw all of those, and above him was the king. The ministries were meant to establish policies for the kingdom as a whole, as well as to manage the territory under direct control of the royal family. They were also in charge of negotiating with the lords of every domain.

The governors held a tremendous amount of power, so negotiating with them took a considerable amount of the ministers' time—and that was on top of their other duties. That was why Alfred was working to centralize the kingdom's power. However, the nobility at large was still too influential for his efforts to have made much of an impact.

Count Sagitalia, the Minister of Finance, had sided with Prince Alfred, along with the Ministers of Defense and Foreign Affairs. But the Ministers of Human Affairs and Infrastructure, along with the Minister of Education, had sided with the second prince.

The seventh player, the Ministry of Education, had been mostly taken over by the Darryl Church. Unfortunately, since the recent scandal during which several high-ranking officials were purged, that branch of the government had descended into a state of chaos. It was, at the moment, largely inactive. As such, Alfred was hoping to separate it from the government wholesale.

The prime minister had maintained his neutrality for a long time, just like the Minister of Law. However, in the wake of his daughter's excommunication, he had decisively thrown his support behind the first prince—or at least, that was how it seemed to those observing the affair.

"The Minister of Human Affairs, guilty of collusion and pocketing funds from the ministry?" Alfred asked as he closed Leticia's report. "Dreadful behavior for someone in his position."

"He's just so fond of jockeying for position with everyone else in the capital." Leticia smirked, and she began to detail just how the minister had spent the embezzled funds first on himself and then to bribe other officials.

"So, while my little brother and I are effectively playing a game of Capture the Flag, there's a round of musical chairs for those vying for power just below us, hm? Seems like a lot of fun we're having."

"That's precisely it. Speaking of which, Brother..."

"Hm? What is it?"

"I'd like you to arrange a meeting with me and Duke Armelia's daughter." Leticia's eyes sparkled, but her tone was so forward that Alfred was momentarily caught off guard.

He had to ask. "A bit out of the blue. Where's this coming from?"

"Well, coming across another woman who works in government is quite rare. I'd love to make her acquaintance. That's merely an excuse, of course; my real reason is because I know just how precious she is to you."

"Letty...my relationship with her isn't what you imagine."

"Oh, isn't it? Then why else have you overlooked all those opportunities to prevent Armelia from gaining more power, especially when you could have done so easily?"

Merellis, the duchess of Armelia, was a favorite of the queen dowager, and consequently, she and her family enjoyed a great deal of influence. As such, it behooved the royal family to keep an eye on them, out of an abundance of caution. Fortunately, House Armelia was the very definition of a noble family; they protected long-held traditions and always put the needs of their citizens first. For that reason, Alfred had thus far never had a problem with them.

"Am I wrong? Or is it that you think you can use her?" Leticia asked sharply, a stubborn gleam in her eye. That look told Alfred that no matter what he said, she would not change her mind.

He let out a sigh. "Even if I said you could meet her, we couldn't invite her here. And you've barely ever set foot outside the capital, much less the palace."

"I'd be safe as long as you and Rudy were with me."

"We'll see."

"That means you're just going to leave me behind again, doesn't it? You're so mean. Isn't he, Rudy?"

Rudy, who had, as ever, been on standby, chuckled at her sudden question. "It's not my place to say."

"Honestly! Not you too, Rudy!" Princess Leticia pouted with disapproval. Then she sighed, and her shoulders dropped. The lighthearted mood darkened in the blink of an eye.

Alfred didn't want to hear what was coming next, but regardless, he held his tongue and listened to what Leticia had to say.

"Enough about Lady Iris. We need to speak, and it's serious. I *must* get outside of this palace. I want to walk through the city as a member of the royal family and see how the people live with my own eyes."

"You still want that, even knowing your position here?" As he asked, Alfred's tone grew naturally firmer.

There were profound limits on Leticia's activities, and she was mostly confined to the royal palace and the castle. This wasn't just because she was a princess and therefore had to be kept cloistered—it was because she so closely resembled their late mother, which had only become more and more apparent as she grew. If the king ever laid eyes on the young woman Leticia had become, he would without a doubt come to dote on her. Therefore, they could not, under any circumstances, allow the king to see her; the more he adored her, the more endangered her life would become.

To say the least, Ellia, the new queen, would not take kindly to seeing the king favor a girl who was the spitting image of the late queen. She regarded both Princess Leticia and Prince Alfred as obstacles. If Leticia ever provoked her, even as a joke, Ellia would doubtless act on the dark feelings she nursed about them both. If that happened, Alfred wasn't sure he would be able to protect his sister. He couldn't be by her side twenty-four hours a day, after all.

Furthermore, Alfred didn't think he could bring himself to trust his own father even in such circumstances. The king had been so heartbroken and lovelorn over their mother...

A wry smile crossed Alfred's face. Perhaps he was just being selfish, keeping his sister shut away. He was afraid to lose her, yes, but more than that, he never wanted to be as powerless as he had been after their mother's death.

Perhaps he had become just as broken as their father. Perhaps that was why he wanted to lock his sister away—so he could lock away his fear of losing her.

"I understand my situation," Leticia said. "And I know that if something dangerous were to happen, I'd just be in the way. But I still want to see the world. If I can't walk in high society, isn't this the least I can do?"

Leticia met Alfred's eyes as she made her case, and he suddenly realized just how much she had grown.

"Please, Brother. I can't live the rest of my life barely ever stepping outside the castle walls and languishing in the palace—not like that *other* brother of mine." The intense light within her eyes spoke to him as well: *If you lock me away, sooner or later, I'll just escape on my own.*

Leticia had come to Alfred to ask for his permission, but at this point, he realized it was just a formality.

"Fine, then," he said.

"What?"

"You want to come have a look around town with me, right? As long as Rudy and I are with you, it should be fine."

"Thank you so much, Brother!" Leticia grinned happily at him. "In that case, I'll hurry and finish looking over the documents I have left. Please finish your work soon, too, so that we can go out right away!"

"All right."

Leticia merrily scooped up a stack of documents that was separate from the ones she had deposited on her brother's desk—the ones he'd been working on and finished just before she came into the room. She gave him one last smile and then left.

Rudius fussed over her as she went, hurrying in her wake. "Ah, Princess! Please, let me carry that for you..."

"You're awfully good, Princess Letty."

"Hm? Whatever do you mean, Rudius?" Leticia asked with a hint of amusement.

You know exactly what I meant, he thought, but he answered her anyway. "That conversation just now. Your goal from the start was to get permission to leave the castle, wasn't it?"

She laughed. "Of course it was."

It left him wondering—did she really want to meet Iris as well? His instinct had told him that Leticia's true purpose had been to get permission to leave the castle. It seemed he was spot-on.

The princess set down the hefty stack of documents on her desk. Her study was smaller than Prince Alfred's. Cute little knickknacks decorated the office here and there, but other than those, the sheer amount of dense, complicated tomes piled on the shelves didn't seem very princess-like at all.

"Don't you remember what my brother always says?" Leticia asked. "When negotiating, first ask for something that they're unlikely to agree to; if you do that, then they're more likely to agree to the thing you really want. And it worked wonderfully!"

Rudius laughed. "So that's why you started out by asking to meet Iris? You're a formidable haggler."

17

Leticia laughed again. "Please don't exaggerate. My brother realized what I was doing about halfway through anyway."

So that was why that complicated look crossed Prince Alfred's face, Rudius thought. It had been when he realized his sister's true aim. Even so, his soft spot for his sister's feelings had led him to play right into her hands.

Leticia took a seat at the beautiful, ornate white desk. In the past, other princesses had probably sat there to write letters. That was the picture the scene painted at first glance, but in the present, the desk was stacked high with official documents.

"Well, I got what I wanted. Surely he can't complain if I just *happen* to run into the young lady of Armelia while wandering through the capital?"

"Ah, that's why you're in such a hurry."

Although the inquiry was over and her part in the church's scandal had come to an end, Iris would likely remain in the capital for a bit longer. Various other incidents had cropped up once the second prince, Edward, insisted on poking his nose into her other affairs.

"Yes. I meant what I said: I want to meet the duke's daughter."

"Why are you so fixated? Although I suppose I can understand the fascination, seeing as she's captured the heart of your beloved brother."

"That's precisely why. But it's not quite the reason you think— I'm not afraid my precious older brother will be taken from me."

In one fell swoop, Leticia guessed Rudius's theory and skewered it. There wasn't much else for him to do but quietly wait for her to continue. Leticia giggled when she saw that she had rendered him speechless.

"Well, of course I'm a tiny bit afraid. But really, I'm more curious about her. Just think about it. My other brother's world is so very small. He's been under Queen Ellia's protection his entire life, surrounded by people who only have good things to say about him. Perhaps that was what led him to break his engagement with the duke's daughter?"

This "other brother" of whom she spoke so derisively was, of course, Prince Edward. Leticia had always referred to him in that manner.

"But in another way, Alfred's world is also small. All he's had is you and me. The only other people he's surrounded himself with are those whom he knows will benefit him in some way."

At last, Rudius began to understand where Leticia was going with all this. It was true that Prince Alfred's world was limited, although in a different way from his younger brother's. He wasn't sheltered, but he was highly selective about whom he accepted into his inner circle. If he deemed a person to be of benefit to him, he would let down his guard, seek their opinions, and chat about all manner of things with them. He was, in short, capable of such intimacy. But at present, the only people he trusted to that degree were his own sister, Leticia, and Rudius.

"Perhaps that's only natural, as a member of the royal family, even if I feel my brother takes it to an extreme. The castle is filled with enemies, and he's shouldered the burden of my protection ever since he was young." Leticia sighed. "I won't dismiss that.

He has quite the mercenary point of view, but he's used those skills to gather the people who work for him. That's part of his strength. But relying on that power leaves him in a precarious situation. To put it simply...he's dependent on loyalty to his results. The second he loses that edge or if he truly slips up, they'll leave him."

Rudius had to agree with her on that. Right now, the only nobles over whom Prince Alfred had any sway were the recently elevated and the provincial lords. They had seen Alfred produce concrete results and were attracted to them. For anyone for whom natural ability was the deciding factor, Alfred was the obvious choice over his brother. However, if Edward ever demonstrated the same potential as his older brother, the nobility wouldn't be persuaded to remain in Alfred's camp because of feelings alone.

"The only reason the neutral faction tipped slightly in Alfred's favor this time was because of Duke Armelia. But *why* did he side with my brother? Is it possible he simply wanted people to think he favored Alfred? House Armelia is so influential that the prime minister could afford to ignore this conflict altogether; the duke could quietly watch us struggle and never make a move, don't you think? Worst-case scenario in this scandal, his daughter would've had to abdicate and withdraw from society. Instead, her father publicly throws his support behind my brother. Why?"

"Do you mean...the prime minister felt he owed the prince?"

"Precisely. Alfred knew that if he backed Lady Iris, he might well divide the country, yet he still chose to help her—even though it didn't directly benefit him to do so."

"And because it wasn't part of one of his own schemes, he could have withdrawn at any point?"

"Yes. But if his eyes are on the end of all this struggle, wouldn't he want to gather as many allies as he could, Rudy?"

"To strengthen the crown, you mean..."

"That's right. He doesn't want to stop at unifying the nobility under his rule, like the kings who came before. He wants to go beyond that. It's a thorny path, but that's why putting himself out there like this is necessary. He doesn't want people who will simply walk beside him; he needs people who will spill their blood for him in times of peace and in times of strife. The military has always adored Dean, admittedly, so I'm sure he won't have trouble on the latter front."

Case in point, Prince Alfred had the loyalty of Rudius, whose grandfather was General Gazell. The general had always had his eye on Alfred, ever since the prince was a young boy. Their relationship had only grown stronger after Alfred secretly joined the military as "Dean."

Those three factors added up to Leticia's hypothesis: The military was incredibly likely to swear allegiance to Prince Alfred once they learned he was Dean.

"To the point, if my brother wants to accelerate the process of strengthening the crown, he also has to strengthen his allegiances. And I was thinking that, in order for that to happen, he needs to step outside of his little world, the one that's just you and me. That was when I learned about Duke Armelia's daughter. She's already expanded Alfred's world, and that made me extremely curious about what kind of person she is."

"Ah, I see. Your Highness?"

"Yes?"

"Are you sure you haven't gone outside the castle already?" Rudius couldn't help but ask. It was hard to believe a member of the royal family could speak so expertly on such things, especially one so young. He smiled wryly. *Normally, anyway...*

"Whatever do you mean?" asked Leticia.

"It's only that you speak of all these things as if you've seen them firsthand, is all."

"It's the opposite, actually. Being kept in this gilded cage, I'm able to describe the state of the outside world so clearly because I so badly want to know about it."

"Ah, is that how it is?"

"Indeed."

That's unfortunate, Rudius thought. Even a dullard could see the potential in Leticia. It was a shame that she hadn't been given a position where she could use it to its fullest extent.

"I still have a great deal to learn, though," said Leticia. "I've never done anything on my own, after all. You can guess all you want about what you'll do in a given situation, but there's really no telling until it actually happens to you."

Rudy wasn't sure about that, in her case. But Princess Leticia always thought much more highly of others than she did of herself. If she gave herself more credit, she might have been less naive to her own ability.

"Back to the point, I was terribly surprised when I saw Alfred take an interest in someone, even going so far as to visit them frequently. Suddenly, someone other than you and I broadens his world, and now he's at her mercy... Rudy?"

"Yes, my lady?"

"Perhaps it's inappropriate for me to ask, since you're related to her, but what do you think about Duke Armelia's daughter? What kind of person is she?"

"A true noble, in both the best and worst senses of the word."

"What do you mean?"

"She is very proud, and she has the strength to walk on her own two feet. That's why the broken engagement didn't destroy her. Instead, she started her own business and began running the duchy."

"I see. So, she and my brother are quite alike, in a way?"

"They are. Her pride means she doesn't like to show any weakness, so she doesn't know how to rely on others. Despite the torment she endured at school, she never lost her composure. She could have done something to retaliate against Lady Yuri's harassment, and she could have even done so subtly—but she didn't. Or she could have asked for support from her family and played the role of the tragic heroine. The people would certainly have seen her in a different light if she had."

Both Rudius and Alfred knew all too well that Lady Yuri had played that card herself, and it had enabled her to boldly cross line after line.

"Lady Iris retains her pride. She has servants who she trusts implicitly, but she still creates boundaries with them. Even if something terrible happens, she refuses to show vulnerability or to cling to them."

"Oh... She really is like my brother. Although, it sounds like she's perhaps a more dedicated and kinder person." Leticia sighed again. "If seeing her close herself off frustrates him to any degree, I hope he takes a good, long look at himself and changes his own ways."

Rudius laughed quietly. "I think she's changed him already. We've never seen him let anyone else in, after all."

Moreover, this was the first time that Prince Alfred had acted in a risky situation without exhaustively weighing the pros and cons. He had even offered himself up as collateral to Father Rafsimons.

"That's true. Say, how far do you think their relationship has progressed?"

"Well, he's only just realized his feelings, and honestly, I'm not entirely sure she reciprocates."

"Oh, my! And has my brother done anything about it?"

"No, I don't think—"

"Honestly, he's just so clueless when it comes to love. Lady Iris seems a bit dense about it as well."

Rudius was about to agree with her but thought better of it. "Well, you have to understand that she has her own reasons for not wanting to open up."

"If my dear brother wants something badly enough, he'll take action. There's no sense covering for him with pretty words."

She was so blunt about it, Rudius didn't quite know what to say.

"It would benefit me greatly if my brother made a move alr— ah, never mind. As his little sister, I support him wholeheartedly."

Rudius pretended he didn't hear her mumble that first part. Sometimes there was safety in silence.

Leticia quietly rose from her chair and walked over to the window, where she looked down at the view below. "Do you remember the first time we met?"

"Yes, of course. Prince Alfred brought me to the castle, and you were hiding behind his back. You were so shy you wouldn't even show me your face."

"That's right," she agreed, an echo of that shyness in her voice. A fond smile crossed her face. "It was so *fun*... Those days truly were just full of delight. We used to play in the garden together, remember? Ever since I was little, I've never been allowed outside the palace walls. I'd barely been outside of the castle, much less into town. So I always looked forward to when Alfred brought you home. He and my grandmother were my entire world...and then you were, too."

"Princess Leticia..."

"Oh, don't make that face. I'm happy. Of course, I wonder what it's like to be part of high society, or what it's like to go to school, or what other young people my age like to chat about. There are quite a lot of things I'd love to know more of..."

The official explanation for Leticia's absence from the public eye had always been that she was sickly. Although she had interacted with a few other children her age, she had never been allowed to attend school. She really had lived her life like a bird in a gilded cage.

"But I understand that all of this was done to protect me. I'm not always sure about Grandmother...but I know that my brother doesn't think of me as a tool. He would never, under any circumstances, try to marry me off against my will. Although I'm sure that's partly because if I had a child, it would complicate things for him."

In truth, Prince Alfred was holding the queen dowager in check from getting Princess Leticia engaged. Even though Prince Edward had successfully kept Prince Alfred away from court, if Princess Leticia had a child, the line of succession would be thrown into even more chaos.

At present, there were only three real candidates in line for the crown: the Princes Alfred and Edward, and the Princess Leticia. The two princes were engaged in battle for that throne, and if Alfred lost, he expected he would die. No one believed that Queen Ellia would settle for something as lenient as his imprisonment.

That was why Prince Alfred couldn't back down from this fight.

On the other hand, if he won, and if Princess Leticia were to wed and have a child, the family of the man she married would almost surely have troublesome thoughts. What if "something" were to happen to Prince Alfred? The next king would come from *their* family...

With that, a new struggle for the throne would begin.

That was why Prince Alfred strove to keep the queen dowager from marrying off his sister.

"Even so, I'm sure his primary reason for keeping me cooped up is to protect me from Queen Ellia's supporters. Once I leave, it will quickly become more difficult to maintain the story of my illness. And if I enter high society, well...my face alone will provoke her, I'm sure. My brother really is protecting me."

"You're that important to him."

Leticia laughed. "So I am. In that case, my marriage will have to wait until after he secures his victory. Ah, although I'm sure if he loses, my *other* brother will marry me off to another country or some such."

A faint flicker of pain raced through Rudius's chest when he heard the princess speak of such a fate. It was only a brief, fleeting ache. Perhaps it was his imagination? He quickly refocused his attention back on the conversation.

"Anyway...whenever I feel anxious or lonely, I just think back on when we were children. It was truly when I was the happiest," Leticia said with a sad smile. It didn't last long before it was replaced with a determined, serious expression. "Rudy, we *must* win. For my brother, and for myself. And for Lady Iris as well."

"I agree."

"For starters, we need to come up with a countermeasure for the trade sanctions against Armelia. Knowing my brother, I'm sure he already has some ideas up his sleeve?"

"Yes, I believe so."

Leticia gave him a smile. "I'll help in any way I can."

Accomplishments *of the* Duke's Daughter

CHAPTER 12

The Duke's Daughter Settles Things

I SAT AT MY DESK in my study. As usual, a tremendous number of documents were piled up on top of it. I'd just finished signing my approval on several of them. Having reached a good stopping point, I decided to take a break and call in Tanya.

"I want to know what's going on with Ed's company."

"I've already looked into it." Tanya handed me a stack of papers.

She never ceases to amaze me, I thought as I flipped through her report. Our sales had suffered since the scandal surrounding my (now rescinded) excommunication. That was true for both the Azuta Corporation and all the companies based in Armelia, to some extent. The timing of Ed's maneuvers had done no small amount of damage to my position both as the president of my company and as the acting governor of my duchy. The proof lay in the mountain of work under which I was presently buried.

To be honest, I hadn't had time to think about all this while I was in the thick of escaping excommunication, but now that it was over, I couldn't stop ruminating over how the pope and Ed's faction had gotten the best of me.

Luckily, we'd defused the situation and taken care of it all quickly enough. However, we were dealing with the loss of not only customers but vital staff members from the Azuta Corporation as well. A shiver went down my spine whenever I thought of what might have happened had we not dealt with the situation so swiftly.

"I'm so glad that Dean was able to connect with Father Rafsimons, and with such perfect timing. Otherwise, Azuta would have either folded or been bought out. Not only that, every business based in Armelia probably would have struggled to remain afloat," I mused.

Tanya nodded in agreement. "I know there's no sense in going on about the what-ifs, but *if* Father Rafsimons hadn't cooperated, we wouldn't have been able to land such a decisive finishing blow. I think you were only able to act as you did because you had that in your back pocket. And *if* we hadn't secured such a solid victory in our favor, the businesses in Armelia would have folded sooner or later."

Moreover, since I'd been focusing on expanding Armelia's economic influence, that would have been a devastating blow indeed. After suffering such a loss, all the owners of those companies would have turned their backs on me. It would have only made sense for them to do so, as they never would have ended up in such dire straits had they not based their businesses in Armelia.

To put it simply, Ed had tried to destroy Armelia not by military force but through targeting our purse strings.

Nevertheless, all those what-ifs had thankfully ended up purely hypothetical, and that future had not come to pass.

In reality, we'd survived the inquiry, and thanks to some new products, business for the Azuta Corporation was on the rebound. The other companies based in the duchy were similarly reporting a gradual return to business as usual.

"Seems like things at Ed's company are getting a bit desperate," I remarked as I read over the documents. Business wasn't going nearly as well for his company as it had been during the scandal. They sold basically the same products that we did, and at the same prices. But since he had headhunted only members of my production crew, we still had far better customer service; the overall quality of our products was better, too. Due to all those factors, the customers we had lost during the scandal had mostly returned.

To make matters worse for Ed, his business was being run so sloppily and was in such a state of confusion that he was losing clients left and right.

"Yes, and because of that, he's been neglecting his employees," Tanya explained. "Now they're losing motivation because of the lack of customers. Some of his people are saying that the employment contracts and the working conditions were much better at Azuta. Furthermore, the business is so bad that they're having to let people go."

"You sound rather blunt about it."

"Do you pity him, my lady?"

"Don't be ridiculous. But...I just think it's a bit of a shame that he went to so much trouble to snipe my employees, only to fire them. Seems like such a waste."

Of course, it made sense to reduce staff when business was bad. Even if you personally hated to do it, as a businessperson, you always had to tuck that away in your mind as a measure of last resort. I couldn't blame him for doing so.

But it was an undeniable fact that his business had outperformed Azuta due to his theft of my employees, even if he had only retained them for a short amount of time. In my opinion, it was therefore particularly cold of him to ignore the results they had produced and fire them just like that.

"People find it difficult to relinquish their economic influence and position in society, especially if they've built it themselves. Consequently, the former Azuta employees who worked for him report that their pay was quite high when they were first hired, but they had numerous complaints about the way they were treated after business went bad. Those complaints were likely the grounds for which they were dismissed."

It seemed like, despite the uncertainty surrounding our financial future during the scandal, the working conditions had remained much better at Azuta. After working for me, my former employees had set their bar a bit high for Ed.

"Have any of Ed's dismissed employees tried to come back to Azuta?"

"I expect they might," Tanya answered promptly, at which I let out a sigh.

It had taken so much time to reconfigure ourselves in the

chaos of their departure, and now I would have to come up with a plan of action in case they came back asking for their old jobs. How much work was this all going to add up to, anyway? Speaking of work...

"I wonder why Ed raised our tariffs?" I murmured out loud. I'd been thinking about this for a while now.

"Most likely for the sole purpose of harassing you," Tanya replied from my side.

"Hmm... While that's definitely possible, I feel like there must be more to it. After all, by doing this, he's definitely introduced more problems for the kingdom than he's solved."

Armelia was a large domain and probably either the second- or third-foremost exporter of goods in the kingdom. Of course, our exports had fallen during the recent scandal, but that also meant that fewer goods were making their way to other domains. Even when we were able to export goods, we weren't turning much of a profit by doing so. Our domain's population was constantly growing, so even without high tariffs, it was less profitable to export our goods than it was to buy up and sell them within our own domain. We needed those stockpiles in case of an emergency, like a poor harvest due to inclement weather.

"I'm thinking about it because we have a dearth of resources at present. I'd like you to find out what the nobles in the capital are up to and report back on their activities. And see what the prices are like within the city and the reactions to them. At any rate, I've done enough for today."

I placed my signature on one last document and handed it to Tanya. Now that I was done with that, perhaps I could walk around the grounds. My body was stiff and painful from sitting in the same position at my desk all day. *Yes, that was just the thing,* I thought as I stood and headed out the door. *Maybe I'll take a book out to the garden and read while I drink some tea.*

Just then, I happened to run into Berne.

"Oh, Berne!"

"What are you up to, Sister?"

"I just finished my work for the day, so I was thinking of taking a break."

"Might I have a minute of your time?" Berne asked.

I flashed him a wry smile. "Is it something that we can discuss in the courtyard?"

He responded with an equally wry smile.

"Well, in that case, shall we go to the study?" I asked. We could drink the tea there.

On second thought, I was sure Tanya was about to send someone to ensure I actually left the study, so I went ahead and took Berne back to my room instead.

"Well? What is it?" I asked once we were there.

"I'm not sure if it's more like I'm asking you for advice or giving you information..." Berne seemed so hesitant that I knew it must be something bad. "The other day, it was suggested to the king that he disband the military."

I was so shocked that I was sure my eyes looked like saucers.

Whatever the expression on my face was, it was certainly not befitting of a duke's daughter.

"Y-you mean that nonsense Yuri Neuer was speaking of a while back? I can't believe it made its way to the king..." I sighed. At the same time, a shiver raced down my spine. I couldn't believe Yuri had so much power now that she was trying to make her foolishness a reality. "I imagine that if the suggestion was made to the king, then it already has the backing of numerous nobles?"

"Yes. The suggestion was made while Father had his hands tied during your excommunication."

That made this at least partly my fault...

"But thankfully, you resolved the situation quickly. Father, Grandfa—er, General Gazell, and others who opposed the idea successfully defeated the measure."

"The measure *was* rejected, then. How?" I asked.

"I heard they used the Wartime Regime Act."

"The Wartime Regime Act?" That sounded vaguely familiar. I tipped my head to the side and tried to dredge up where I could've heard it before. I suddenly remembered I had seen it in a book in the library back at the mansion. "Oh, that outdated old edict...?"

It was as old as the kingdom itself. Just as the name suggested, it was a law that took effect during wartime. It had only been used once in several hundred years and never since. It had been soon after the kingdom's founding, back when each domain was even more autonomous. At the time, the kingdom had maintained no permanent military unto itself; instead, each domain sent soldiers to aid the king as needed. The law was invoked against the rulers of domains who opposed the kingdom's wars to the point that they refused to send soldiers—the act forced them to do so. Then, after the war, those rulers were at risk of having their domains reclaimed by the crown.

As a consequence, the king had established a permanent military under the crown to avoid this ever happening. Each domain nevertheless kept a certain number of soldiers beholden only to them under the guise of self-defense.

To wit, the reason this act had never been enforced since that first incident several hundred years ago was because there had been no need for it. Now that there was a permanent standing military, anytime war threatened the kingdom, the nobility had agreed to face the enemy as one and the kingdom had united. In other words, the fact that the act had been invoked now showed just how divided the kingdom had become.

"We only have a cease-fire agreement with Tweil, so technically the war isn't over. Thus, since we are at war, the act is valid and can be applied, correct?"

"Yes, that's right."

"Father must have had a difficult time with this. But I'm relieved he was able to avoid having the military disbanded. That would have been the absolute worst-case scenario."

That was putting it lightly, to be honest. As Father had said, we *were* still technically at war. Moreover, having investigated Yuri Neuer's past, I knew that Tweil was making aggressive moves behind the scenes. But as my father had warned me, at the end of the day, I was still only a governor. I had no intention of responding to their aggression in kind.

"Yes, but..." Berne started.

"There's more?"

"No, I just wanted your advice on something. Father has given me homework on the matter."

"What do you mean?"

"Well, he asked me to identify the biggest problem in this situation."

"The biggest problem, hm... And?"

"I was just thinking perhaps I could run it by you, and if anything came to mind, you might give me a hint."

"And Father asked you to give me this message?"

"Yes."

I thought about it for a moment. If my hunch was correct, Father wanted to pass along this information not as a father to his daughter but as the current governor of Armelia to the acting governor of Armelia. In other words, he was telling me to ready myself.

"Berne, which nobles backed the proposal of military disbandment to the king?"

"Primarily those belonging to the second prince's faction. Some members of the neutral party, too. I thought the problem might be that the neutral families are being swayed toward the second prince's side..."

"And he told you that wasn't it?"

"Yes."

I asked Berne to name the families that had agreed with the military disbandment. After I heard them, I looked up at the ceiling and thought, *Ah, this country is on the brink...*

"And the plan was that if the measure was approved, the newly unemployed soldiers would be provided with relief?"

"Yes. It would have depended on the desires of every given person, but in times of peace, they would have been reemployed as domain-specific troops. But in case of emergency, they would be drafted to serve under the crown itself. So in the end, the domains would share the burden of our current military expenditures."

Ah, I knew it. I let out a sigh. "Berne, I'm not sure if I'm right about this, but I have a feeling that Father wants to see how deeply you can think on a problem that has no clear answer—what predictions you can make and how you act on those predictions."

In the course of this job, I'd thought so many times that it would be so much easier if every problem had a clear solution like on a test at school, however...

Berne frowned. "I see..."

"The neutral families have started to lean toward the second prince's faction, hm? Well. That *is* a problem. But is that the true issue, I wonder?"

"What do you mean?"

"I'm telling you to think about the situation from all possible angles. On what basis did the neutral faction support this measure, and what desirable outcome did they foresee? Mull that over. There's no right or wrong answer, so just teasing out reasons and consequences will help you prepare a countermeasure for every possible scenario."

Berne paused thoughtfully to consider what I'd said, and then he nodded. "Thank you, Sister."

"Of course. And thank you for the information."

I noticed as he left that the expression on his face looked much more at ease than when he'd first come into the room.

Seconds after my brother departed, Tanya came in, followed by Lyle and Dida. Perfect timing.

"I'm sorry to spring this on you right after you've returned, Tanya, but I need you to prepare a report on the duchy's stock-piles at once. Meanwhile, Lyle, Dida, I want a report on the current number of soldiers in our garrison, as well as how many private soldiers there are in Armelia as a whole. I want numbers on potential commanders as well."

Tanya bowed her head. "Yes, my lady."

Lyle and Dida followed suit, but Dida had a question. "We'll get on that right away, but...did something happen, Princess?"

This was awfully sudden, so I didn't blame him.

"Berne just gave me a message from my father," I explained. "A proposal was made to the king, suggesting that he should disband the kingdom's military."

"What?!" All three of them gasped in unison, equally shocked.

I was sure their concerns were partly for Armelia's citizens, but they were also worried about my grandfather, their master, who was the general of the army.

"Luckily, my father and grandfather put a stop to it."

All three of them breathed a sigh of relief.

"But the problem is how this all came to pass in the first place—the people who proposed it and the content of the proposal itself."

"What do you mean?"

"I'll preface this by saying that it's merely my own opinion. I could be wrong." They all nodded. "Let's begin at the beginning. I have a feeling the person who started all this was Yuri Neuer."

"That woman..." Lyle didn't even try to hide his disdain. It was extremely rare for him to show any of his emotions so openly, let alone negative ones.

"I'm not sure how she did it—though judging from Tanya's report, I have a suspicion that she's connected to Tweil."

But how closely, and where had it begun? Perhaps someone was threatening her. Or maybe she was being used without her knowledge? Who knew—maybe she was the mastermind behind the whole operation after all. We knew nothing for certain; I didn't even have concrete evidence of her link to Tweil. Whatever the case, I would do well to think through the situation from the viewpoint of the worst-case scenario.

"While my father's hands were tied due to my mistakes, the king was approached about disbanding the military. It was exactly what Tweil would have wanted. Looking back on it now, I have to wonder whether someone, maybe even Yuri herself, was puppeting the Darryl Church in order to attack me and to thereby incapacitate my father."

That would make the most sense. The pope had been

extremely intent on my excommunication—so much so that I had to wonder if he had been promised a handsome reward in exchange.

I could almost hear the frustration steaming off of my three companions as I voiced my theory.

"But our problem going forward will be the people who agreed with the proposal," I said.

"The second prince's faction, I'm sure?" Lyle asked, just as I had expected him to.

"Yes, but that's not all. This time, a few members of the neutral faction decided they agreed as well."

"What? They did?" Lyle sounded genuinely surprised. Meanwhile, Tanya and Dida wore grave looks.

"But how could that benefit them?" Lyle asked.

"I think they hope to lawfully expand their own garrisons."

"What do you mean?"

"Well, Lyle and Dida...as you know, the ruler of each domain is only allowed to keep the bare minimum number of soldiers, determined by the size of their domain."

These were the last vestiges of a time when the provincial rulers had wielded more power. A number of problems had arisen from competing military strengths, and forming one large army under the crown had been a compromise in that regard. We still enjoyed that arrangement today.

"Since then, the governors have always kept each other in check. And the kingdom keeps a watchful eye on any domain that seems to be amassing too much military force."

They did this in order to prevent any one domain from splitting off from the kingdom.

"Another proposal was brought up at the same time as the one to disband the military. They suggested that the crown divide the released soldiers between the domains, and as a consequence, every ruler would share the burden of overall military expenses. In case of war, the soldiers would return to fight on behalf of the kingdom. However, doing this would naturally return us to an age when the domains held an enormous amount of power. I can imagine quite a few families belonging to the neutral faction would welcome this, which means..."

"They want military strength in case something happens." Dida finished my sentence for me. "But to put it more frankly... they're turning their back on the kingdom?"

"Yes. Although I'm not sure if they actively want to split off from Tasmeria or if they just want to shore up their own domains."

"And you want us to check on our own forces in case we have to fight them, Princess?" Dida asked. "Are you thinking of being both the sword and shield for the crown?"

"Of course not. I just want to be prepared, is all. What with all the troubles both at home and abroad, I want to ensure we can protect Armelia when the time comes."

Lyle remained unusually silent, perhaps still shocked by the revelation of the proposals.

"Hmm... But..." Dida, meanwhile, sounded like his usual easygoing self, yet I could tell that he was serious. "The person who orders the soldiers to assemble in case of an emergency—

that'd be the acting governor. In other words, it would be you, Princess."

"Yes, that's right."

At least, that's what I thought would happen. Father would be busy spending his energy on the central government. Even so, if he'd been without my assistance as the acting governor, for such an important decision, I'm sure he would have sent personal orders from the capital, even if it took longer for those orders to arrive. Sebastian had run the general affairs of the duchy for a long time and to great success, but my father had never granted him the authority to give such orders. However, that wouldn't be a concern with me, since I possessed all the powers an actual governor would have.

At any rate, if a prompt response was necessary, it would be better to have more authority than I intended to use than otherwise.

"Are you prepared for that, Princess?" Dida's look was incredibly stern. "War means killing. It means getting hurt and possibly even dying yourself. One word from you, and that's the situation you'd be putting your soldiers in."

"Dida," Lyle interjected sharply.

Dida brushed him off. "Are you really prepared to give orders for people to kill and be killed, Princess?"

"Dida!"

Lyle's shout echoed. For a moment, the room fell deathly silent.

"Everyone must be prepared if we go to war," said Lyle. "Prepared to lose our lives, hold a sword, and have our own two hands stained with the blood of our enemies. There's no reason for Lady Iris to shoulder that burden all on her own." His voice was quiet yet so firm that it resounded. I had, for a split second, almost faltered until I heard the affection in his tone.

"Sure. I'm prepared for it, too," said Dida. "But you don't have the resolve necessary for the bloody bits, do you, Princess? That said, with one word, you send us out to the battlefield. Even if you won't be there giving us orders directly, your words will be our guide. Our lives, and the lives of our citizens, will be in your hands. You'd be responsible for everyone standing out on that field, and in the aftermath as well. Isn't that right?"

Dida looked at me. Lyle had shut his mouth.

"Even if you never raise a hand to anyone, the mere act of signing the orders puts blood on your hands."

Dida was right. And his words had skewered my heart, which throbbed with pain.

I couldn't pretend I was ignorant, no matter what the citizens thought of me. Everything could change with one order. Even if our ultimate reasons for going to war were to protect the people, by giving the order to fight, I would be sentencing many of them to their deaths. One word of mine really could mean life or the lack of it. I would also be involving citizens who didn't *want* war.

If violence did break out, could I give the orders to fight?

"I'm not telling you that you have to be ready for that right now, Princess. But if you're going to order us to prepare for such a scenario, then you'd best prepare yourself for what lies ahead, too."

I had told myself the same thing, but I didn't yet have an answer.

"You're right, Dida." My voice sounded incredibly pathetic, but there was nothing I could do about it. Because it *was* pathetic. Here I was, telling Dida and Lyle to ready themselves, and I wasn't ready at all. "I can't answer your question yet. I need more time."

"All right. At any rate, we'll get that report ready for you."

I was surprised by Dida's response; I had assumed that he would say he wouldn't act until I could give him an answer.

"Very well..." I said. "I look forward to it."

Dida and Lyle excused themselves, so I resumed my work. But I just couldn't get that conversation out of my head.

"Ah!" And as a result, I made a mistake on the document I was working on. I was simply unable to concentrate. I set down my pen and stretched my arms high. My stiff joints cracked so loudly, it was hard to believe the sound was coming from the arms of a young girl. Still, all I could think of was that conversation.

There was no right answer.

The same thought had run through my head many times since I had become the acting governor. Once again, I'd hit that same wall. It was easy to let go of the fact if the problem was hypothetical. I could just tell myself I'd have to make my mind up when the time came, and that would be that.

Dida wouldn't be satisfied with such a wishy-washy response. Moreover, I knew that any bravado I used to cover up my true feelings would only fall apart at the eleventh hour. When that time came...I would no longer be able to lie to myself. In fact, I was afraid that I would completely lose my composure.

Up until this point, I'd been responsible for many fates, many lives. An incompetent leader got their citizens killed. But this matter was on a whole different level. People would be giving and taking lives, and I would be directly responsible for every last one. That put the lives of my citizens in my hands even more so than ever before.

It was such an immense responsibility that my former self would have shrunk away from it. I felt like I was doing the same thing now, for that matter.

If only no one ever had to get hurt.

No, that thought was only a pretense. The real problem was that I was afraid to give the order.

If only I were really just inside of a game, I thought. Then perhaps there might be a perfect world where everyone was only ever kind to one another. No one would get hurt, and all the unsavory details would be brushed over like in a fairy tale or seen through rose-colored glasses.

Then again, even in the game, Iris had been a villain who assumed single-handed responsibility for all the bad things that had happened. So really, there had never been a world where everyone was ever-so-kind. And *this* world was my reality. If it weren't, its harshness wouldn't be staring me in the face.

In the jumble of my thoughts, I found myself circling the dirty tricks I'd seen the nobility play in their political games and the incredible disparity between the rich and the poor—neither of which had been remotely highlighted in the game's story. More thoughts like this popped into my head, one after another. I couldn't stop *thinking*.

I should have Tanya bring me something to drink. There was no way I could keep working in this state. I was just about to call for Tanya when the mountain of papers on my desk collapsed. Sheets flew haphazardly up into the air. *Ah, now I've really done it!*

I'd spent so much time separating the documents, and now they were all mixed up again. Just thinking about the time and effort it would take to put them back in order made me upset.

"Tanya," I called.

"Yes, I'm here."

"I'm sorry, but I'm going to the parlor. Please have the maids prepare some tea for me. And can I ask you to straighten up these documents for me?"

"Of course."

Thus did I end up abandoning everything and taking a break to leisurely sip tea by myself in the parlor. The beautiful flower arrangements usually cheered me up when I was feeling down, but nothing could reach me where I was.

I let out a deep sigh.

"Why, Iris! Whatever is the matter? You look so depressed!" My mother suddenly appeared, her voice sweet and cheerful.

"Mother..."

"I'll have what Iris is having," she told a maid before sitting down across from me. "Taking a break?"

"Yes... I'm a little tired."

"It's no good to bottle things up. Honestly, you're just like your grandfather." Mother was even beautiful when she giggled, and so was the movement of her hand as she brought the teacup to her mouth. I found myself staring at her sometimes, purely because she was so lovely—even though she was my own mother. "Are you sure it's only fatigue? Because it seems like something is on your mind."

I stiffened with surprise. Was I that obvious?

"Iris, let's go outside. You start to think about all the worst things when you're cooped up indoors for too long," she declared, grabbing my hand and pulling me out of the room.

"What? Huh?" I blubbered as my mother dragged me along. She was stronger than she looked. I turned back and saw the maids all in a flutter.

Mother instructed me to get into the carriage waiting outside. Sometime later, I found myself following her up a long staircase in a tower so tall that you could look out over the entire capital from its top.

"It's gorgeous..." I murmured, marveling at the stunning view. The blue sky seemed close enough to touch, and the light of the sun gently embraced me. The city looked more beautiful than I'd ever seen it, bathed in the golden light.

"Yes, it is beautiful, Iris."

"What is this place, Mother?"

"A watchtower for the capital's guards. I believe it still belongs to the military."

"Well then, I'm surprised we're allowed up here." After all, it was a military facility. Even though we were nobles, we were still civilians and therefore generally not permitted in such spaces.

"An easy feat when I use my father's name." I was in awe of

my mother's breezy tone. She smiled. "Ever since I was a child, I would come up here whenever I was worried about something. So all the guards recognize me."

"What kind of things worried you, Mother?"

She laughed. "Oh, like when your father and I would get into a fight, or when he beat me when we sparred during martial arts class." Her voice was always so light and airy. "And I also came here when my dream was shattered."

"Your dream? What are you talking about?" I couldn't even imagine what Mother's dream could be. She was called the Flower of High Society and prided herself in her elegance. She seemed like the kind of person who truly had it all. I had no idea what dream she could have had that she would've given up on.

"Long ago, I wanted to become a soldier."

That was the last thing I'd expected her to say, and my eyes widened with surprise. "A soldier?"

"Yes. I took martial arts lessons from the time I was very young, after my mother had been killed by bandits."

I had never heard this story before, and my shock grew all the more.

"My father's grief was immense. There he was, the man who had won so many victories on the battlefield and secured peace for the kingdom, yet he had been unable to protect his own wife. Not only that, but it was a citizen who he'd helped to protect who had stolen her away. It was unthinkable."

Hurt squeezed my chest. My grandfather was a legendary war hero. A savior on the battlefield. But he had been unable to save my grandmother when she was killed by a citizen whom he had himself rescued from death.

"So, when my mother died, I began learning martial arts. Father didn't object, because of what had happened to Mother. I didn't learn the etiquette most young noblewomen do. Instead, I was a tomboy who yearned to become a soldier."

I kept thinking I couldn't be more shocked, yet I was. How many times had my mother surprised me in this one conversation? I mean, this was my mother we were talking about! The lady everyone called the epitome of all noblewomen. I couldn't believe she hadn't learned etiquette until—who knew when!

"I'm not sure if it was because Father was such a good teacher or if it was as he said—that I just had a talent for it—but I never lost to any of his students, whether they were my age or older. The only one I can ever remember losing to was Father." She giggled softly, but I couldn't bring myself to join her. "So, at some point, I decided I wanted to become a soldier like him and protect the kingdom."

"But the person who killed Grandmother was a citizen of Tasmeria, right? So then why..."

"It's true. I hated the bandit who killed my mother, and at first, I couldn't understand why my father still wanted to protect this kingdom. I'm not sure if I was driven by hatred or if I just wanted to learn how to protect myself. Honestly, I don't know what I was thinking when I first started training."

Suddenly, a darkness entered my mother's smile. But it was only for a fleeting moment, and it was soon erased by the sun.

"I suppose that's why I felt so empty when Father was the one who caught the bandit responsible for killing my mother. I wondered why I had spent so much time training. I lost my sense of purpose. And I came here to think about that a great deal. Why *had* I picked up a sword? I thought and thought, and thanks to this view, I put my mind and heart in order." She gestured to the view below as if to say, *See?*

There were so many people in the beautiful city below.

"There are people in every one of those buildings. They go about their daily business. They laugh and they cry. They can do all those things because they're alive. And I thought, isn't that such a marvelous, wonderful thing?"

"Mother..."

"Of course, there are wicked people out there, like that bandit. But there are even more helpless citizens. I wanted to make sure that they never had to endure a sudden tragedy like my family and I had. I wanted this peaceful land to last forever. I wanted to protect them, even if it meant getting blood on my hands."

Hearing my mother's resolve shook me to my core. "You were that determined at such a young age?"

"Well, I had lost someone precious to me. I think perhaps that I had a very strong desire to never lose someone like that again."

"Mother..."

"But reality didn't bend my way. Women aren't allowed in the military, even today. A few men I beat at a tournament confronted me with that bitter truth. With that, my dreams shattered into a million pieces, right then and there."

What fragile little men they were, I thought, angry even though it had happened so long ago. But it was because of the hurt that I had lived through that I could empathize with what my mother had experienced back then.

"Did you ever want to become a knight?" I asked.

Some women were allowed to become knights in order to protect the women in the royal family.

"I didn't pick up a sword so I could protect the crown. And honestly, the lady knights are more for show than anything."

I had to agree. Although the lady knights of Tasmeria underwent a certain amount of training, they rarely saw any real action. They were never sent into battle for the same reason that the military didn't send any women into the line of fire.

"So, when that happened, I came up here again. But it didn't help. Because the goal I'd held for so long had vanished into thin air."

Mother had no one left to take her revenge on, and the dream she'd forged in its place had been snatched away. I suddenly felt ashamed for ever thinking that Mother was the kind of person who'd always gotten what she wanted.

"And that's where I met my husband. Right here."

"You did?"

"Yes. At the time, his father was the prime minister. He discovered this place on a tour of the capital, and he was so enamored with the view that he often came here just as I did."

For a moment, I worried over how lax the security was in this place. I supposed it was fine, as no one had been hurt, but still...

"So there I was, crying my eyes out, and your father just ignored me and kept staring out at the view—as if I was ruining the mood at his favorite thinking spot. Even though I was embarrassed, I took out my frustrations on him." My mother's cheeks turned pink—it sounded as if this had been the beginning of their romance, so I was starting to feel a bit shy hearing about it, too. "But you know how your father is. He scolded me."

"He did?!"

"That's right. He said, 'You must not have wanted it very badly at all if you're giving up so easily.'"

I couldn't believe Father had said that to a poor, crying girl! I had to wonder why Mother looked so happy telling me the story.

"He said, 'Why did you take up your sword in the first place? Was it for honor and glory, or was it to protect the citizens? If it's the former, then keep crying. But if it's the latter, then why in the world would you cry at all?'"

"'Why would you cry at all?'"

"Mm-hmm. I think what he was trying to say was 'There's another way to achieve your goal.'"

Ah, I understood. If Mother's dream had been to become a soldier to fight and earn honor and glory, then her dreams had been completely dashed. But if her goal was to protect the citizens...

"He said, 'If you want to protect the citizens, you have more than one way of doing so. You can support them in other ways. In my case, I protect them not with my sword but with my pen.

Although, I'm not nearly as skilled at it as my father.'" Mother smiled. "His words shook me. It felt as if I'd just woken up. After that, we entered an arranged marriage. But I respected him so much that I quickly fell in love. We got married, and then I decided to set foot on another type of battleground."

"Oh?"

"Yes. The battleground of high society is a completely different beast." She said that with a smile so proud and bright that I had to laugh in return.

She was right. It *was* a battleground. Perhaps she had become so powerful on that field because she had grown strong by experiencing real fighting. She used her husband's network to gain information and leveraged his power to gather more goodwill and influence for herself.

"Thank you for bringing me here today, Mother. May we stay and look at the view for a bit longer?"

"Of course."

Once we got home, I climbed into bed prepared to fall into a deep sleep right away. But I was wide awake and couldn't drift off. I couldn't stop thinking about my conversation with my mother and the view from the watchtower.

"I wanted to make sure that they never had to endure such a sudden tragedy like my family and I had. I wanted this peaceful land to last forever."

The look on her face had been so heartbreakingly lovely when she said that. And I don't mean her physical beauty—more like the tender, caring serenity of a mother.

How did I feel about my citizens? I thought back on everything I'd done so far. I couldn't help but laugh—because it was the same thing.

When I'd met Mina and the other children from the orphanage—no, it had started before that, when I was touring the duchy and had made up my mind. I'd never governed before, obviously. But I'd been granted power under the title of acting governor. The lives of all my citizens depended on every step I took, every decision I made. I felt the weight of responsibility for every single document that passed across my desk. I did that work to protect those lives.

I already had my resolve, didn't I?

It seemed that my brush with excommunication had made me soft. I'd been worried that perhaps having me as a leader had put Armelia at a dreadful disadvantage and that everything I did would leave the duchy in ruins.

Those thoughts had run through my mind, even though it was no time to be bogged down by such a mindset. I had to power through. The citizens and the entire duchy were already wrapped up in my affairs. It was far too late to say I wasn't prepared. If I wanted my plans to come to fruition, my only option was, as ever, to keep going. I could *not* lose sight of my goal.

If I faltered now, then so too would the people who had chosen to follow me, and all the citizens under my protection as well. So I had to do everything in my power to protect them.

All at once, the knot of anxiety inside me unraveled. At last, I fell into a peaceful, dream-filled sleep.

The next day, I called Lyle and Dida to my study.

"How may we be at your service, Princess?"

"I've made a decision," I told them.

Lyle's eyes widened, and Dida gave me an amused grin.

"Dida, you asked me yesterday if I was prepared."

"That I did."

"I know I hesitated when you asked me that, but I've thought about it, and hard. I realize now that you should have asked me that question a long time ago." Dida stared at me blankly as I spoke. "Because I've been prepared to protect the citizens of this duchy from the very beginning."

"So much that you'd spill blood to protect them?"

"Yes...and no."

Now it was Lyle's turn to look puzzled.

I smiled grimly. "I already hold thousands of lives in my hands. My role is to protect the duchy and its people. So, if the time comes when it is necessary to give the orders to mobilize our soldiers, then of course I will. And I will take responsibility for all that comes with that decision."

There was no perfect world in which no one ever got hurt. I had known that from the beginning.

"But I'm going to fight with everything I have to ensure that doesn't happen. I have no wish for us to get swept up in the un-folding struggles. I'm not thinking about how to win a war—I'm thinking of how to avoid one in the first place. I will be making my first move toward that end."

"If you want to protect the citizens, you have more than one way of doing so."

Those words, which my father had said to my mother long ago, applied to me right now.

I'd been so caught up in thinking about what I would do if war broke out and how I would take responsibility for it. How would I respond as the acting governor? But that wasn't what I should have been focusing on. There was more than one way for me to deal with this. I could anticipate what would happen next, gather intelligence, and prepare countermeasures for every possible outcome. My greatest weapons were my pen, my head, and my words. Military force would always be the last resort, only to be used once I had played all the other cards in my hand. That was my responsibility as the acting governor.

"But if I decide that there is no other way forward but to fight... Lyle, Dida, I'll be counting on you to ensure that the bare minimum of blood is spilled. And I will take full responsibility for having exhausted all other options," I said firmly.

For some reason, Dida started to laugh. Had I said something funny? I thought this was all terribly serious.

"That's a wonderful resolve you have, and said in the sweetest way possible."

"Dida!" Lyle exclaimed indignantly.

"But it's fine. That's why we have such a strong desire to protect you, Princess. You, and the things precious to you."

Had I passed his test?

"Why don't you just be honest with your feelings for once?" Lyle said with exasperation. "My lady, we shall serve as your shield and your sword. We shall deliver you from every fear. And if fear is all you have left, please let us be your bastion. We shall protect you no matter what. You, and the things precious to you."

He gave me the knight's salute. Dida assumed the same position by his side.

"Thank you, Lyle and Dida."

If they still didn't want to lose me—if they still wanted to protect me—then I had to do everything I could to fight.

While I was racking my brain coming up with plans, Sei had been busy at work addressing the sudden raise in import taxes that had lately plagued Armelia. Meanwhile, I started maneuvering against the companies under Prince Edward's protection. All of his businesses were suffering from poor sales and management. Not only that, but the person managing the companies was involved in dodgy dealings and tried to usurp the valid successor to take complete control.

I had my people work behind the scenes to worsen the business's already dreadful condition, and when their hands were tied, we had the board oust the shady manager and reinstate the rightful successor. Then, we approached the new head of the company with a contract.

The business would keep its name, but it would take over all shipping for the Azuta Corporation's goods. You see, the increased tariffs only applied to businesses based in Armelia. In other words, if this non-Armelian business shipped our goods for us, we would only be taxed the standard rate. Other Armelian-based businesses had approached non-Armelian companies with similar contracts.

This worked nicely for us in a number of ways; it was one thing to cut costs by dodging high tariffs, but now we wouldn't have to cover the costs of hiring guards for the trade caravans either.

I gave out the initial orders, but afterward, I had Sei work alone to finish things up. He'd really come to the rescue this time.

None of this solved the underlying problem, though. It was now on me to standardize the tariffs laid on us by our neighboring domains. It would by no means be easy.

It was clear to me that our neighbors had raised tariffs for reasons outside of pure economics. However, even if they had resisted whatever political pressure had been put on them to do this, the second queen, who had directed them, would remain in power. She would eagerly seize the next opportunity to crush us.

I was the daughter of the prime minister, but neither I nor the territorial governors possessed ultimate authority. The only person who did was the king—although the king was currently ill and indisposed.

Even if he'd been well, I don't know that he could have done anything. The governors controlled regional tariffs. Even in times of peace, when the king could leverage his ultimate authority in a number of ways, he still had no say over those.

In other words, the regional lords were being controlled by other means, and I had to deal with that.

At any rate, I had done what I set out to do, so it was time to return to the duchy. Even though Sebastian was skilled at his work, there would inevitably be a backlog of documents awaiting my approval.

Ah, but it might not be so bad if only Dean were there to help, I thought as I straightened up the paperwork.

"Tanya, I'm thinking of returning to the duchy," I said.

"I think that's an excellent idea. I'll get everything arranged."

Ah, that's right. I had to say the proper goodbyes and tie up all my loose ends here in the capital, so I wouldn't be able to leave right away. "Thank you."

I missed Armelia. It wasn't like I'd been away for years, like I had when I was in school. But for some reason, it felt like I hadn't been home in a very long time. I supposed that was partially because of how busy my days in the capital had been.

"My lady, you've received a letter from Lady Mimosa."

I took the letter from Tanya and broke the seal with my letter opener. I felt like I was much better at speed-reading than I had been.

Just then, there was a knock at the door. Tanya went ahead and opened it. As she stood there and spoke with the servant who was behind it, her expression grew more and more severe.

"Send him away at once."

"But..."

Tanya's voice was cold and forceful. The servant sounded a bit frightened but didn't back down.

"Fine. I'll go instead," Tanya snapped, ending the conversation. However, the servant looked thoroughly relieved to hear that.

Who in the world could be calling who would warrant such a reaction? I frowned. "Tanya?"

"Excuse me, my lady. I'll deal with this." Her tone made it clear that she didn't want me to know who it was; she hoped to take care of it before I found out.

But if someone had come to visit me, I *had* to know who.

"Wait, Tanya. Who's here?"

"You needn't concern yourself with it, my lady. I'll take care of everything."

"Tanya." I said her name more firmly this time, and she let out a sigh.

"Van Lutasha has come to see you."

"Van?" I had certainly never expected to hear that name, and I was honestly a bit flustered.

"You shouldn't see him while Lyle and Dida are away. Who knows what he might have up his sleeve? Not to mention, it's beyond rude to visit without contacting us first."

That was true, especially as I'd never actually had a conversation with him before. He hadn't wanted to hear me out when I was in trouble, so why *should* I listen to what he had to say?

I nodded. "All right. I'll let you take care of it, then."

"Thank you."

Even so, what in the world was Van doing here? I was so curious, I could hardly stand it. Did it have something to do with my recent brush with excommunication? As a consequence of that, Van's father, the former pope, had been released from his duties and thrown in jail. I would have thought he would visit anyone else in the world before me.

For starters, Yuri Neuer had gained a great deal of influence since her engagement to Ed. After all, he was the second prince, and his grandfather was Marquis Marea, who prided himself in having so much power that his wishes became law nearly as soon as he imagined them.

On the other hand, it would have been difficult for Van to meet Berne, as my brother had been spending so much time working under Father. Likewise, Dorssen seemed rather busy since joining the knights. But, well, my schedule was pretty packed, too.

I just wanted to finish my business and go home. Surely Van wouldn't come all the way to Armelia to see me. What would he even say if he saw me? The mere thought of it irritated me.

"I've returned, my lady." Tanya entered the room again.

"That was awfully fast."

"Yes. He left." Her tone was derisive, but her face was utterly composed. She had to have been exceptionally irritated. I would have to reward her later.

But first, the important questions: "What did he say?"

"Not a thing—because I chased him out of here before he could even open his mouth." Tanya was smiling, but her eyes were not. In fact, the aura she emanated was so icy that I grew chilly, and goosebumps rose all down my arms. I wanted to ask exactly *how* she had chased him off, but frankly, I was too afraid.

Well, I'm sure she wouldn't do anything too *bad.* At least, I hoped she wouldn't. "All right, then. Me sitting here thinking about it isn't going to accomplish anything. Will you straighten up those documents for me?"

"Yes, of course." This time, she responded with a genuine smile.

"And I want you to look into what's going on with Van."

"I will."

Tanya had become quite the spy. Of course, House Armelia had numerous people whose main occupation was espionage, but she did a better job of it, if you asked me.

To be more precise, those other individuals worked for my father. But after my tussle with the church and everything that had come with it, I'd realized just how precious information could be; I had started gathering spies who were loyal specifically to me. It was difficult to find people you could trust so completely, so I had only a few thus far. I therefore had to heavily rely on my parents' and grandfather's connections.

"Let's hurry up and finish our work here so we can go home."

"Yes, my lady."

But before I left the capital, I went out on the town. I didn't have much time, but since I was there, I wanted to clear my mind for a bit and do some shopping purely for pleasure. I could also buy some presents to take back to everyone who had remained at the duchy.

"What should I get them, though?"

I imagined Rehme and Moneda would like some kind of sweets, the kind one could only find in the capital. Their work was so cerebral, so eating something sweet would refresh their minds. However, both Merida and Sei spent a lot of time in the kitchen, so sweets didn't seem appropriate for them...

"I'm sure they'll love whatever you choose, my lady," Tanya said, to which I chuckled wryly.

"That makes it even more difficult! If I'm giving them a present, I want it to be something they want, or at least something they can use."

I was slightly disguised as we walked through town, just as usual. I narrowed down the shops to a few I particularly wanted to visit. I was still mulling over the perfect gifts to get everyone when I suddenly spotted someone familiar.

"Hm? Dean?" I couldn't believe it was really him. A woman was walking with him. What was he doing here? And who was *she*?

A jumble of confused thoughts ran through my head, and a feeling of uneasiness wound around my heart.

Well, I supposed Dean was free to be wherever he wanted, and with whomever he wanted. I couldn't deny that in my head, but the anxiety in my heart simply wouldn't go away. I felt utterly childish. I had to laugh at the jealousy welling within me; it had come seemingly out of nowhere—I was surprised.

When Dean noticed me, a matching look of surprise flashed across his face. Even that reaction annoyed me. Did he not want to see me? Was I an interruption? Although, I supposed that under normal circumstances, it was always awkward to run into your boss outside of the workplace.

Well. I wasn't having fun anymore. *Time to go home.*

Tragically, it would have looked terribly unnatural if I just turned on my heel and walked in the opposite direction—and I hadn't bought the presents yet either.

"It's good to see you again, my lady." Dean greeted me. Did he feel an obligation to do so since we had made eye contact?

"It's been a long time, Dean. I wasn't expecting to run into you in the capital. And who is this?" I tried my very best to smile as I asked, but honestly, I wasn't confident it was successful.

The beautiful girl standing next to Dean smiled far more brightly, her eyes shining. "It's a pleasure to meet you. My name is Letty. I've heard so much about you from my brother."

"Your brother?" Now that I looked at them more closely, it all made sense. Letty *did* look very much like Dean. The only difference was that Dean's eyes were emerald green, but hers were a bright peridot color.

"Yes, that's right. My family is very overprotective of me, so I'm not allowed to go out by myself. And when my brother goes to visit you, I'm the one who takes over his work. I'm so sorry I haven't been able to meet you sooner."

Ah, then I owe her some gratitude for helping me out, by extension. I should thank her. I hadn't said my name yet...but it would have been a bad idea to do so openly, out here in the street. "Your brother has been an invaluable assistant, time and again. Please forgive me for being unable to properly introduce myself in these circumstances."

"Not at all! I understand your position, my lady. Actually, I've been yearning to sit down and have a nice long talk with you. I want to make sure my brother is pulling his weight for you." Letty's smile reminded me of nothing so much as a flower in full bloom.

"My lady, please dismiss my sister. I know you're dreadfully busy, and I can't imagine you'd have time to talk to—"

"Are you afraid she'll tell me something bad about you, Brother?"

"Letty! What am I going to do with you?"

I was amused to see Dean react so unusually; he looked flustered, unsure of what to do. I had never seen him like this before.

"Oh, my!" I couldn't help but laugh.

Letty glanced over at me and giggled as well.

"It's fine with me," I told her. "But let's find somewhere else to talk."

Thus, we made our way to a nearby restaurant. The establishment was run by an Armelian business, so we secured a private room right away.

"Please allow me to formally introduce myself," I said once we were seated. "I am Iris Lana Armelia."

"It's a pleasure to make your acquaintance," Letty said with a smile.

"Dean really has helped me out so much. I'm sorry he's always leaving you to come help me."

"It's quite all right. I like the work. But most of all, I deeply respect you, so I enjoy every minute of it."

"You do?" I couldn't hide my surprise. Letty had never even met me before. How could she respect me? But her eyes were sparkling so much that I had a hard time believing she was only saying that to be polite.

"I heard that the economic reforms you initiated in Armelia once you became acting governor were simply remarkable. And I've heard of so many people who relocated to Armelia because the quality of life is so much better there now. I truly respect your abilities. But most of all, it makes me so happy to have a conversation with a woman who's out there on the front lines."

She spoke as if she could read my thoughts. She was young, and she was adorable, but yes—she was definitely Dean's sister, all right.

"Thank you. Shall I take that to mean you have an occupation as well? What sort of responsibilities does it entail?"

"I mainly pen my brother's documents and sift through various bits of information. I also do some behind-the-scenes maneuvering for negotiations that would've come to my brother, I suppose you could say? It isn't so much that I take over his work, but I *am* always helping him put his work together and getting it executed the way he likes."

"You're too humble. It takes patience and perseverance to compose documentation, as well as to use the knowledge you've gained to influence negotiations. Even in my work as the acting governor, the bulk of my job is creating and sorting through documents. We're basically doing a lot of the same things!"

"Ah, but in your case, you make important decisions and take responsibility for them. That's completely different from what I do. I'm sincerely flattered, nevertheless."

We continued talking for some time, and I found myself thoroughly enjoying my time with Letty.

"What?! You've had that happen, too, Lady Iris?!"

"Yes, several times. After you spend so many hours buried in documents, your head feels so heavy!"

"I know... It's especially bad the next morning if you've worked all night."

"Yes, same for me!"

We had come to the topic of our health woes and were trading ways to combat stress. Quite unusual topics of conversation for most young maidens, to be sure. I always felt like the girls my age preferred talking about love and trendy bakeries or some such.

It was evident from our conversation that Letty really was doing Dean's work and not just saying so; we were able to commiserate about our worries because we shared so many of them. In fact, we were so absorbed in our discussion that we ended up completely ignoring poor Dean.

There was a lull in our talk, and abruptly, the smile vanished from Letty's face, replaced by a somber expression. "Lady Iris, I only assist my brother, but from my perspective, it seems as if you do the work of two or three people. Perhaps you should let someone lighten your workload, as I do for my brother?"

"I've lightened it as much as I can, I'm afraid. I have employees I trust to help with the corporation, and I have loyal assistants who work under me managing the duchy—and that includes your brother."

"And is my brother truly helpful?"

"Absolutely. He's profoundly attentive to detail and does such careful work. If not for him, I would have collapsed from overwork long ago."

I meant everything I said; Dean was truly my right-hand man. It was difficult for me to express in words, but I felt like he could carry out my instructions just as well as, or even better than, Sebastian, Sei, Rehme—even Tanya.

It was only natural that being in their positions, they would do their utmost to follow my instructions to the letter. Dean, on the other hand, wasn't bound by the same feelings. That was why he could give me his honest opinions. He'd hear me out when I rattled off an idea that popped into my head, help me organize and streamline my thoughts, tell me just how much of the idea was actually feasible, and then give me another opinion to work off of.

As a result, I was able to work more quickly and efficiently, since I didn't have to mull over all of the complications by myself.

"Is that right? I suppose he does pay attention to the fine details. That's why I can't slack off even a little bit when I do work for him..."

I had to laugh at that.

"Letty, at least say those things when I'm not around," Dean sighed. It was the first thing he'd said since our conversation began.

"Oh, Dean, who knows when I might see Lady Iris again? I have to tell her everything that's on my mind right away!"

"You mentioned you're not allowed to go out much?" I asked.

"Yes. My family truly is overprotective. And since my brother travels so much, if I took too much time off, my work would just pile up and cause all sorts of trouble for those who work below me."

"I see. Do you normally stay in the capital, then?"

"Indeed, I do."

"Well, I'm sure I'll be back. I'll make sure we see each other then."

"My lady, we ought to be going..." Tanya informed me reluctantly.

Time really does fly when you're having fun.

"I'm terribly sorry I kept you for so long, Lady Iris," said Letty. "Please let me know when you come back to the capital."

"Yes, of course. And I'll visit those places you recommended." In the course of our conversation, Letty had told me of several shops that were especially fashionable at the moment. I intended to visit them to find those gifts I wanted for everyone back home.

"I hope you find some wonderful presents."

"Thank you. Dean? I'll be waiting for you back in the duchy."

He nodded. "Yes. I just need to finish tying up some business here, and then I'll see you in Armelia."

"All right."

With that, I left to resume my search for the gifts. I had to buy them on this trip, as we were leaving the capital the next day.

I ended up purchasing handkerchiefs for Merida and Sei, and sweets for the rest of the crew.

I was feeling quite satisfied with my purchases on the carriage ride home, but my good mood was dashed as soon as we returned to the mansion and I saw who awaited me there.

"Lady Iris!" He cried my name and raced over to me. Lyle and Dida then stepped in front of me protectively. "I've been wanting to see you! Lady Iris, please listen to me!"

I knew the man, of course. "Van... What are you doing here?"

Lyle and Dida tensed when I said his name. Van looked distressed, likely because Tanya had already chased him off once.

"Why?" he asked. "Because there's something I need to talk to you about! Before, they told me you weren't home and sent me away, but today, I decided to wait for you."

"This is beyond rude, Van!" Tanya snarled. "Showing up here without notice! How dare you disrespect House Armelia in such a way?!"

Lyle and Dida didn't speak, but I could tell they were thinking the same thing. They looked *furious*.

"Fine, then," I said. "We can't be seen like this, so come along inside."

"Lady Iris!"

"I've no interest in causing any more of a commotion out here. I'll hear what you have to say, Van. Inside." I realized my tone was short, but I didn't respond well to people who just showed up unannounced on my doorstep. I heaved an irritated sigh and entered the mansion.

"Quite strict around here, aren't you?" said Van once we were in my study. From the moment he set foot in the mansion, he had been received with caution and hostility. As we walked, Lyle, Dida, and Tanya had remained at my side to protect me.

"Did you think you would be welcomed with open arms?" I asked.

"No, my apologies."

"Well? What was it you wanted to say? I'm returning to Armelia tomorrow, so I'd appreciate it if you kept this short."

"I have a favor to ask of you."

"Yes?" Granted, I had asked him to keep it short, but I was surprised by this sudden request. Really, how dare he ask a favor of me at all?

Pure malice radiated from my three escorts; it was like they wanted to pounce on him and would do so at the least provocation.

"I want you to give testimony for me."

"Excuse me?" I'd suspected Van would say something to that effect, but I hadn't imagined he would actually be so bold.

"I know it's shameless to ask this of you after all the trouble I caused you, but I'm in a terrible position. The Darryl Church is in a state of complete chaos. I fear its troubles will ripple out and impact all of Tasmeria. I understand that my father was the one who instigated this chaos, and that you were his victim—but that means that if we could demonstrate a cooperative spirit, we might just be able to prevent the situation from worsening."

Van was right in saying that the Darryl Church was on unstable ground, following the imprisonment of the former pope and other high-ranking officials who had been held responsible for conspiracy. I had heard that the nobles known to collude with the pope and his faction were also currently under investigation. In reality, those nobles were scapegoats. They were all minor figures—not the masterminds behind the whole thing.

"It's true that the chaos within the church will negatively impact the kingdom," I said.

"In that case..." Van looked at me hopefully.

But too bad for you. I leveled a stare at him and asked icily, "However, how could it possibly be to my advantage to cooperate with you?"

"Advantage?" Van repeated the word as if he didn't know what it meant.

"Yes. *Advantage.* If I cooperate with you, what's in it for me?"

"Shouldn't your first priority as a noble be to save the kingdom from all possible danger?"

"How amusing. Am I correct in saying none of this ever would have happened had the church not falsely accused me?" I laughed—a laugh that came from deep in my belly. "It's a little late to be concerned about the kingdom's stability. At present, the nobility is divided into two factions arguing over who should be the next king. Well, three actually, if you count the neutral faction. If this situation drags out any longer, it will be a miracle in and of itself if Tasmeria survives at all."

I didn't know how to keep it intact, though I respected the people who were trying to do so. If the power struggle spread, it would affect the citizen's daily lives. If that happened, it would be no surprise if a neighboring country took advantage of our internal strife to wage an attack. In short, it would be commendable indeed if anyone were able to nip our succession crisis in the bud.

Perhaps it was presumptuous of me to compare running a domain to governing a whole kingdom, but I was without a doubt the most skilled governor in Tasmeria. No one opposed me in Armelia, so I could push forward any new policies I wanted without disruption—I was the beginning and end of the chain of command.

But a kingdom is different; you must always consider how to protect yourself from the forces who oppose your actions, wonder if or when your allies will betray you, and doubt whether they were ever truly your allies in the first place. Despite all that, you must strive to run things smoothly. Add a stressful environment on top of that, and you have a dreadful job—one where, and this would be no exaggeration, one wrong step could lead you to endanger the royal family.

Hm, maybe I should give my father some heartburn medication.

All these thoughts ran through my head as I stared at Van. "You were party to worsening that divide, and now you're saying you want to save the kingdom from falling into chaos by joining forces with me? Where is this coming from?"

"I didn't do anything to endanger the kingdom."

"Ah, you're naive, then? You really are awfully close to Prince Edward," I said with a derisive chuckle.

That must have hit him where it hurt, because he frowned. "We went to the same school. It's only natural we'd be close."

"It's *not* only natural, and that's why I say it. The academy is a microcosm of aristocratic society. It would be *natural* for you to cleave to the same faction your parents support. I don't know whether it was the prince's favor you were courting or Yuri's, but after seeing you grow so cozy, anyone would think that you, and by extension your father, supported Prince Edward."

Honestly, Berne and I had behaved injudiciously as well. Normally, upon my engagement to the prince, Berne should have distanced himself from Ed, but instead, Berne had grown closer to him through Yuri. I understood now how my father had felt when he'd given me that lecture after I was expelled—or at least, I understood him now even more than I had then.

"You exacerbated the power struggle in this kingdom. So having you come to me, saying you want to better this country? All I can do is laugh."

Van closed his eyes for a moment. When he opened them, a deeply pained expression was carved onto his face. Had I gone too far? "I'm fully aware of my impudence. That's exactly why I must take responsibility for my actions. I want to do everything I can to ensure the situation doesn't spiral out of control."

"And your first step is trying to join me?"

Van hesitated a bit and then nodded.

I take that back—I didn't go too far at all. I heaved a sigh at his heel-turn. All I could do after was let out a dry laugh. "It's inevitable that things would be messy before a major revolution. Especially when the leaders of the old regime are not only ousted but arrested." I closed my fan with a snap. "Quite frankly, the corruption within the church was unacceptable. You pocketed money you collected from the nobles instead of distributing it to the citizens."

"The clergy needs to make a living, too. And—"

"If you say it can't be helped, you can turn around and get out of my house right now."

Van's face tightened at my menacing tone.

"A non-insignificant sum flowed from taxes straight back into the church," I said. "Do you have any idea how much effort it took to collect that money in the first place?"

Our tax collectors did *not* have an easy job. Not only did they have to manage sums, they also had to assign a reasonable rate to every citizen. It was an incredibly difficult task. As the acting governor, I couldn't overlook Van's blasé attitude about the money our citizens paid to sustain our society.

"As if that wasn't enough," I went on, "think of all the donations you collected, all the charity galas you held. Where in the world did all that money go?"

"Well..." Van looked uneasy, as if he wanted to say he didn't know. But he must have realized that if he did say as much, I would lose it, because he quickly shut his mouth.

"I didn't know"—I could have said those same words so many times in the past. Until I had regained the memories of my past life, I'd taken my station for granted and never questioned anything. Even now, I wasn't sure whether I could hold my head high and say I was fulfilling my responsibilities as a noble. At the very least, I was now more aware of my surroundings. That was a fact.

"The church abused its power. My excommunication is a clear example of that. Yes, our political state is fraught as a consequence of uncovering its deceptions, but if that means the church can no longer interfere with the business of running our kingdom, then that's a win for Tasmeria. It is a far more concrete good than me making much of cooperating with another noble to create the illusion of peace."

Van bit his lip and looked downward.

"Thus, no, I will not cooperate with you. You may excuse yourself." I rose from my seat, a signal for him to leave.

"Please, wait!" Van stepped toward me, and Tanya, Lyle, and Dida all stood in his way.

"Is there something else?"

"I—I only...!" As he stammered and pleaded, I found myself looking indifferently at him. "What should I do?! Please help me!"

Help him, hm? I had to laugh. "And why should I help you?"

"Because..."

"I'm the *villainess* who abused *poor, kind* Yuri, remember? You and Prince Edward publicly denounced me. So why in the world would I ever help you—without good reason?"

My voice was so cold that it actually surprised me. I could clearly hear Van begging me for help, but I didn't care. I felt neither sympathy nor pity, not even satisfaction that the tables had turned. I just felt nothing.

It made me realize just how insignificant Van was to me.

"My father had the papacy taken from him. I thought Yuri wouldn't care, but she suddenly started acting like I didn't exist. She treated me as if I were invisible!"

In other words, Yuri had only ever wanted Van for the power he held through the church. To be honest, hearing his plight only made me more impressed with her. I'm sure it had felt wonderfully refreshing to be able to cut ties with him so cleanly.

"Everyone else in my life has suddenly changed as well—they treat me so callously. I..."

"So what?" I asked flatly. "The person you love is acting like you don't exist? Everyone else turned their backs on you and is treating you like an inconvenience? I honestly don't care—because *you* didn't care when it happened to me, correct?"

His face twisted at my sarcastic tone. "Yes, you're right. And I understand I'm partly responsible for getting you expelled. Even I think I'm a true idiot for coming here because of that."

"Oh, so you *do* understand! Wonderful! Now leave."

"But I can't give up. I want revenge on all the people who turned on me. I don't want this to end with me doing nothing!" he screamed.

I laughed.

Van had always been so kind and gentle—he sure had changed. I took in the man in front of me, his face contorted with rage as he seethed. He clung to his rage, despite knowing he had no chance to really find satisfaction; I simply couldn't believe he was that same person I had known back at the academy.

"Fine, you're right," he snarled. "If I'm being honest, I don't care about the kingdom. I came to you because I want revenge on those who abandoned me!"

"Well? Say you get revenge—then what? Beg for Yuri's love? Plead for the others to stay by your side?"

"No. They've abandoned me. I don't care about them at all, not anymore. I just want to do this for my own sake!"

How incredibly self-serving. But I couldn't dismiss him out of hand, because I knew what that felt like. After everything I'd endured, I had certainly felt the desire to get revenge. However, that was what made this situation precarious.

There was a defining difference between Van and me: Revenge wasn't my driving goal. The citizens were what kept me from growing too attached to the idea. As I looked at Van, it was clear that he felt no such impediment. There was only one thing on his mind, and it was all he wanted. Even more dangerously, I got the feeling that he would stop at nothing in order to achieve his goal.

I sat back down across from him. "So that's why you really want to join forces with me?"

Van nodded. It made sense now; he had guessed that I also nursed a desire to have my revenge, and so, of all his options, he had chosen me.

Unfortunately for him, it just wouldn't work out.

"No amount of pushing from me will get you the papacy. The church is already being restructured from the ground up."

I'd been discussing the matter with Father Rafsimons, and according to his report, there was no way Van could ever become pope. First of all, nearly every high-ranking member of the church had not only been ousted; they had been thrown in jail. Now the majority opinion was that the cardinals should choose the next pope from among themselves.

"Honestly, instead of backing you, I'd rather support Father Rafsimons, since he's being so very shrewd about all this. Not only do you no longer have the backing of the church, you're also inexperienced in all other matters. At this point, it will be incredibly difficult for you to remain with the organization in any capacity."

Van's position was hanging by a thread. If not for this incident, he would have entered the main church in the capital to undergo training as the next pope and gained his experience there. Now they wanted to do away with hereditary succession. Moreover, they were doing everything they could to wash away the old regime, so Van's existence was worse than an obstruction—the church wanted absolutely nothing to do with him. I honestly wondered if they'd even let him continue being a member of the clergy.

"However, I could place you at an acquaintance's church," I said. "As a regular clergyman, of course."

I could certainly ask Father Rafiel for this favor. We had a personal connection, and I trusted his abilities. Of course, this would all depend on whether or not Father Rafiel agreed to it.

"Keep in mind, this is only a *clergyman* position. It will be a far cry from becoming pope, and I'm not sure if you'd ever be able to work at the main church. But the people in this church trust what they see with their own eyes instead of the rumors they hear. If you hone your skills and show what you're made of, it's possible they'll warm up to you, and you might earn a higher appointment."

What would Van do?

The answer: He didn't show any hesitation whatsoever.

We exchanged a written agreement, and he left.

"Why did you show him such kindness?" Lyle asked, sounding none too happy about it. I thought it interesting that Tanya hadn't been the first to speak up, but I understood as soon as I saw the understanding on her face.

"Was it kindness?" I asked with a chuckle. Lyle gave me a puzzled look. "Tanya, prepare letters for both Father Rafsimons and Father Rafiel right away."

"Yes, my lady," Tanya responded.

"As I told Van, the Darryl Church is undergoing a complete restructuring. That doesn't mean everyone agrees with it, as I'm sure you can imagine." The high-ranking clergymen hadn't been the only ones lining their pockets with donations—their noble sponsors had benefited as well. I doubted in the extreme that they were just sitting on their hands while they watched the church be upended. They were absolutely going to try to disrupt the proceedings.

It was entirely possible that those people would try to use Van's lineage and his vulnerable state to their advantage, even raising him up as a banner around which to rally. That was why I wanted Van on my side—before any others could take him away.

"He's going to use his frustration as fuel, and that's when my assistance will come in handy. Father Rafsimons will tell me what

Van's up to so I can use him to my advantage. Moreover, nothing I told Van was a lie. Father Rafiel went to medical school in order to serve the citizens. His philosophies overlap with Father Rafsimons's, and if Van works with him, he might well open up a new path to the main church for himself. If he does, I can call in the debt he owes me when it's time."

I was doing all this because I believed in Father Rafsimons's power.

"On the other hand, if Van abandons his quest for revenge, then that's fine as well. I'll know what he's up to, and I'll have countermeasures ready in advance for anything. If he steps out of line, I'll know immediately." I smiled. "Also, if I take care of Van, Father Rafsimons will owe me a favor."

"I see..." Lyle nodded. "In that case, I'll keep an eye on him and those he keeps close."

"I was just thinking about asking you to do so. No matter how the situation turns out, I benefit from it. Do you still think I was showing him kindness?"

The moment Van came asking me for a favor, I'd known that it would end up benefiting me. I could laugh about it forever. And what was wrong with that? I was the villainess in this story, but Van had chosen to come to me, even if as a last resort.

Tanya let out a sigh once she finished brushing her hair.

It was nearly midnight. Iris had fallen fast asleep, and since then, Tanya had been busy getting things ready to depart. Now that she was finally done, she was about to go to sleep herself.

Sometimes Iris would half-jokingly ask her, "What? You actually sleep?" But Tanya was only human. She nevertheless did find herself wondering the same thing about Sebastian from time to time. He never showed any signs of fatigue and always had a pleasant look on his face, which impressed her. She strove to be like him.

These piecemeal thoughts flitted through Tanya's head as she reached down and picked up a ribbon from her desk. She, Rehme, Merida, and Iris all had matching ribbons. She couldn't recall exactly when they had gotten them. Probably before she had even begun training to be a maid.

A traveling merchant had come through Armelia and had asked Iris if she wanted anything.

"Are you sure? Not the one with the gemstones?" Duke Armelia had looked bewildered when Iris chose a relatively plain ribbon instead of the fancier, more expensive options. Duchess Armelia had also encouraged her to choose a more fitting accessory.

"No, I want this one. And I want four of them."

Once Iris had the four ribbons, she passed out three of them to her girl companions.

"Now we all match," she had said with a smile.

To Tanya, the ribbon was expensive, but to the daughter of a duke like Iris, it was dirt cheap. Yet she spoke of it as if it were a treasure.

"I'm sorry if it's not what you would've chosen," said Iris. "I just wanted us all to have the same one. I hope you'll accept it."

The ribbons were priceless treasures to the three girls—because they were heartfelt gifts from Iris. Tanya truly felt fortunate. Luck had led her to be at that place and time where Iris found her. If they hadn't met, Tanya would surely have died.

She didn't know how long she had been left alone. She had most likely been abandoned by her parents, left to fend for herself in the slums of the city where the most destitute gathered. Being so young and so helpless, there were many days when Tanya had nothing to eat. Gradually, she had grown weaker and weaker.

Some days back then, all Tanya could do was sit on the ground and look up at the sky. Sometimes she saw a mother and child walking hand in hand through town, and an overwhelming urge to cry would well up in her chest. It didn't take long at all for Tanya to begin wondering: If she was just going to die alone, then should she just give up on living at all? She began to wish she could hurry up and get it over with—that she could disappear forever.

Then one fateful day, two men Tanya had never seen before approached her. She didn't remember what they had said, but she instinctively knew by the coaxing smiles on their faces that these men were no friends. Even though she had all but given up on living, her body reacted to imminent danger. She got up and ran.

Tanya ran and ran, but a frail little girl whose body was weak from malnourishment couldn't run for very long. The men closed in, about to catch her.

Then Iris saved her. Tanya was blindly running, but she happened to end up on the main street. She bolted out into it, right in front of Iris's carriage.

"Are you all right?"

The carriage halted, Iris rushed out from it, and Tanya knew instantly they were from two entirely different worlds. She managed to nod at this alien girl.

"I'm so glad! Hey...is there somewhere we can take you?"

Tanya shook her head.

"Oh. Well, why don't you come home with me?"

"No. It doesn't matter. You saved me—that's enough. I can't trouble you again. I got away from them this time, but...there's nothing else to be done."

"Don't—don't give up on yourself."

After that, Iris insisted on taking Tanya home with her, even though her servants tried to convince her otherwise.

That was how Iris saved her.

"It just seemed like you were in so much danger," Iris had said. "I told my father about those men."

Tanya only learned later that the men who had approached her made their money by kidnapping orphans and selling them off as slaves for cheap. They gave up on Tanya after they saw Iris and her servants making a fuss, but thanks to Iris's description of the men, they were soon apprehended and arrested.

"Starting today, you're going to be living here with us," Iris said. "What's your name?"

"I...don't know."

"All right, then. What do you think about Tanya? It's the name of a very clever princess in a fairy tale book."

Iris reached out and clutched Tanya's hand, sunshine illuminating her smile. The warmth of her hand reminded Tanya of the families she had seen walking by her when she was huddled alone on the streets. Big, fat tears began to stream down her face, and she couldn't make them stop.

"O-oh, do you not like it? I can pick a different name!" Iris panicked as Tanya began to sob.

Tanya thought it funny, but she still couldn't stop crying. Iris had saved her in more than one way. Not only had Iris saved Tanya from danger, she had also given Tanya a reason to live when she had given up on herself.

That was why Tanya never wanted Iris to worry. In fact, she wanted to protect Iris from everything that could possibly concern her. She had prayed that Iris would be able to return home to Armelia soon; she hadn't seen a genuine smile on Iris's face since they arrived at the capital. Her mistress only ever looked exhausted.

That was understandable, given the scandal they had been dealing with upon their arrival. Furthermore, Iris had been consumed by negotiations and damage control in the aftermath. It was no wonder that she had been so tense.

So, yes, it was understandable, yet Iris had that gloomy look even in private.

"Did something happen to Lady Iris?" Dean had asked Tanya before he left with his sister. He showed up so infrequently, yet even he had noticed her mood.

All the other maids of the house had seen it as well. They were all too aware, but they couldn't do a thing to help. That was incredibly frustrating for Tanya, especially as she couldn't identify what could have upset Iris so terribly.

She had a hunch, granted. She suspected it was simply being *here*, in the place where Iris had been humiliated. Worse, upon Iris's return to the capital, she had been subjected to yet more humiliation. Could anyone really wonder why she was so upset to be here?

For whatever reason, Iris simply couldn't be herself in this place. It was almost as if she was *trying* to make herself look bad.

True, Iris was no longer the ray of sunshine she had been when she was little. She had grown up, of course. Moreover, Tanya was a servant, and she had no need to develop political insight, but even she knew that the old Iris never would have been able to survive the scheming and machinations of high society. Other people would have made her a puppet or taken advantage of her.

Therefore, it was necessary for Iris to keep her cool and not let her personal feelings interfere with the difficult decisions before her. But that coolness was even more pronounced in the capital. Her bright, sunny smile had been replaced by a cold, unfeeling one.

Again, Tanya felt like Iris was almost trying to make herself look the villain. She had a feeling that Iris was unconsciously aware of it. It seemed to her that the true reason Iris wanted so badly to go home wasn't the work piling up on her desk in Armelia—she wanted to go home because she couldn't stand to be herself any longer. It was almost like she was sick of acting the part. All Tanya could do was hope they would be able to return without further incident.

There was a knock at the door. Tanya went to open it. She was surprised to see Dida standing there. "What are you doing here so late?"

"Sorry about that. Were you about to bed down?"

"Yes. Lady Iris fell asleep quickly tonight, and I've finished all my work for the day."

"I see. Hey, you really shouldn't answer the door wearing that. You *are* a woman, after all."

"Oh? I thought there was no need to worry in the duke's mansion." Tanya smiled. "And of course, I know what to do if someone tries anything with me."

Dida chuckled wryly, but a serious expression came to his face. "What would you do if he was too strong for you? It would take a lot more than what you've got to get through a guy like me."

"Yes... Well, speaking in terms of people in this household, it would be difficult for me to overpower you or Lyle. But if there were an intruder, I think they'd be more interested in trying to kill me than anything else. Either way, I trust the both of you to see to it."

The two of them stared evenly at each other for a few moments. It was the dead of night, and the house was grave quiet; it made the silence between them all the weightier.

"Damn. Guess you got me there," Dida said with a chuckle.

Tanya laughed. "Well? What did you want?"

"I was going to ask Lyle for a drink, but he fell asleep. I was wondering if you'd join me."

"Honestly, at this time of night? Especially after lecturing me about how I should be more careful as a delicate woman? Don't come crying to me if someone sees and starts spreading rumors."

"I don't care," he said with a laugh.

Tanya couldn't tell if he was serious, and she sighed.

"Well, it is late. Bet you gotta get up early tomorrow, too. Sorry," he apologized.

"Wait." Tanya called out to him just as he was about to leave. "I'm wide awake now. Let's go ahead and have that drink. Can you wait a bit for me to change first?"

"Sure."

Tanya went ahead and changed, then left her room to join Dida. It was too late to go out, so instead they used the parlor reserved for the servants. It was a common space used by all the mansion staff, mainly for breaks.

House Armelia's mansion in the capital was appropriate for such a prominent family, and thus, it was so large that about half of it was dedicated space for the staff. This went to show just how highly they valued their staff, and it all made life as a servant to House Armelia quite pleasant.

"What'll you have? I brought this, if you're interested."

"Isn't this from Macalama? How did you get it?"

"Swiped it from Master," Dida said without a trace of remorse.

Tanya sighed. "Honestly. What am I going to do with you?"

"Who cares? Master feels bad about what happened with me

and Lyle. I told him this would make us even, and he laughed." Dida had a wry smile as he spoke.

What an awfully masculine way to show concern, thought Tanya absently, but she silently accepted the glass Dida handed her. "Are you sure it's all right for me to share it, then? Seeing as you earned it through your hard work."

"Lyle said he didn't want any. I wouldn't say it was hard work, anyway."

Tanya doubted that as she watched Dida pour a second glass. She knew how hard General Gazell worked the two of them every time they met. They had given up their own training time to teach the other recruits as the general's assistants. Meanwhile, they continued to serve as Iris's bodyguards, as well as helping to conduct joint training exercises in their free time.

Tanya had barely seen either of them lately, which was likely due to the fact that they were so busy. She'd told them they didn't have to help with House Armelia's domestic needs in the meantime, but Lyle had refused to listen, and Dida had said breezily, "We're just hanging out when we're there."

Tanya and Dida raised their filled glasses and clinked them together. "Cheers."

They both took a sip, and the sweet, deep flavor of the alcohol spread through their mouths.

"Mm, booze from the Macalama region is so damn delicious."

"Isn't it, though. You really lucked out, getting a hold of this."

"All the master's got is the good stuff. For someone who drinks so much, he's real picky about what he likes. Or maybe that's *why* he's so picky. He drinks like a fish!" Dida laughed as he downed the rest of his glass. Then he murmured, "We can finally go home."

"Yes. So now you're done spending your time at the general's."

"Yeah. Gotta start getting ready."

"Are you eager to return as well?" she asked, glancing over at him.

"What do you mean, 'as well'?"

"Nothing in particular. Well, are you?"

"I don't really have a place to call home. When it comes down to it, my home, or I guess the place where I belong, is by the princess's side. So I guess it seems weird to say we're going 'home' anywhere in specific."

"True enough."

Dida had also devoted his life to Iris, just like Tanya. Unfortunately, his easygoing attitude often brought his dedication into question.

"I do wanna go back to the duchy, though. As soon as possible, with our princess. There are too many walls here. I can't be by her side all the time like I can in Armelia. Too many people in the capital have more power than us."

"I have a hard time imagining there are many individuals stronger than you two," Tanya said in a teasing tone, prompting Dida to laugh. He gave her a look that said, *I know, right?*

"I'm joking," Tanya said with a sigh. "It's true that being here makes one feel powerless. So many people have a greater power than we can ever possess—that of influence. No matter how much we train our bodies and blades, we can never match it."

"Right. And that's why I wanna go back to Armelia as soon as we can, as the princess's protectors."

"Yes..."

"You don't look too happy. One of the nobles say something mean to you? The head maid work you too hard for once?"

"Would you say that in front of Elulu?"

Dida gave a throaty chuckle. "Hell no."

Tanya sighed again. "No, that's not what happened. I've just been worried."

"Only thing you'd be worrying about is the princess."

Tanya glared at him. "You sound rather confident about that."

"Well, *pardon me*!" Dida laughed.

Only then did Tanya realize how indignant her response had been, and she let out yet another sigh. "You're right, though. I am worried about her."

"Did something happen?" Dida's voice was suddenly serious. Iris was as important to him as she was to Tanya, and that reminder filled Tanya with relief.

"Haven't you noticed that she's been looking increasingly depressed the longer we stay here?"

"Well, yeah," he agreed with a snort.

"She's always tense, so it's no wonder she's grown this upset. It's just frustrating to see her like that and be unable to do anything to help. It's like what you said—being faced with something more powerful that we can't overcome. I feel like I was overconfident in my own abilities." The more Tanya spoke, the worse that bitter feeling inside became. She had to chuckle at herself.

94

"Yeah, but what about it? Everyone has their strengths and weaknesses."

"I know that. And that's why I'm so frustrated!"

Tanya was up against a wall she couldn't even begin to climb, and she was so weak before it. Being aware of her helplessness made it feel even more insurmountable.

Dida shook his head. "You *don't* know. Lemme give you an example. My specialty is being the princess's bodyguard. I physically shield her body because my role is to protect her. That's my specialty, and I'm better at it than anyone. I won't let anyone take that away from me. Not even you."

Tanya glared at him, still incensed—how dare he say she didn't understand!

"So then what's *your* specialty? Your role is to always be by her side and help her with everything she needs, right? I can't do that. I can't make tea like you can or help her get dressed. I can't manage her schedule or help her with her work either."

"Well, that might be true, but..."

"I know how hard you work. You trained with the master to learn martial arts, and Sebastian taught you how to help with Princess's actual work. I can see that you're trying to expand your role even further. That's fine if it helps her. But there's only so much that one person can do. Everyone has their limits. What's wrong with focusing on taking care of the things she already needs help with? You can grow stronger in your specialty by seeing to those responsibilities."

Dida tipped back his head and drained the last of his drink. "Think I'm wrong?"

"No. No, but..."

Tanya felt like she had just been smacked in the head with a blunt object. She hadn't been overconfident in her abilities at all. She had been too proud—too controlling. She'd thought she had to do everything herself.

Lyle and Dida improved their skills by training with their swords, Merida practiced her cooking, and Rehme always studied to increase her knowledge. Sei and Moneda likewise always worked hard to finish all the tasks they had been given. All of them had their own roles and worked hard to fulfill them, even going above and beyond in the tasks they had been assigned.

"You see what I mean?" asked Dida. "Instead of getting frustrated when you run up against something you can't knock down, figure out what you *can* do for our princess and help her over there."

Tanya drained the last of her drink as well. "You're right. The best I can do to put her at ease is to stay beside her at every moment."

She still had dignity in her role. And just like how Dida said he wouldn't let anyone else take his position, Tanya wouldn't give up hers either.

"That's the look I'm used to," Dida said with his usual full laugh.

CHAPTER 13

The Duke's Daughter
Returns Home

"I'M FINALLY HOME," I murmured to myself. A dozen feelings blurred together within my chest.

It had been so long. Although this trip had been nothing compared to the usual social season, it had felt like forever—likely because each day had been packed with so many developments. The last time I'd returned to Armelia, I had felt no small amount of relief, but this time, it was even greater.

As soon as we arrived back at the mansion, the staff greeted us warmly. "Welcome home!" They were all smiling happy tears. I even began tearing up a bit myself. It was evident that they had all been truly worried about me.

"I'm so happy you're back home safely," said Sebastian. "Please go ahead and rest up from your travels."

"Thanks, Sebastian."

Normally, I would have headed straight for my study, but that day, I went directly to my bedroom. Everyone was right—I needed to rest.

First, I relaxed with a cup of tea that Tanya made me. A gentle breeze rustled the curtains. It seemed to beckon me over, so I rose and walked toward the window, from where I looked out over Armelia. My beautiful domain.

It was lush and green, and I could see the town off in the distance. I loved this view. When I thought of how generations of governors had looked out at this same stretch of land and at the people they protected, I was proud of the blood flowing through my veins. I let out an absent sigh. I was so relieved that I had overcome this crisis and that this land was still my responsibility.

"Oh, that's right—Tanya, could you call Lyle or Dida in here, please?"

"Of course. Are you going somewhere?"

"Yes, but not off the grounds. Don't worry."

"All right, then. Please wait a moment." Tanya excused herself from the room but returned promptly. "Dida just happened to be outside."

"Thank you, Tanya. Dida, would you accompany me on a walk, please?"

"Of course. Where would you like to go?"

"To see my grandfather."

"Oh, that's all? Got it. It's my job to take you wherever you want, Princess."

"Thanks. Tanya, can you get the flowers ready? Would you please come with us?"

"Of course. Please wait a moment and I'll get them ready right away."

With their company, I made my way to the back end of the estate. It took about ten minutes to walk there through the thick woods. These woods were the final resting place for the governors who had passed on. Not in a cemetery, but here. I didn't know the reason why. I was, in any case, somewhat envious that they were able to enjoy their eternal slumber on the land belonging to House Armelia, which was filled with so many memories.

My goal was the newest headstone. I took the bouquet from Tanya and set it on the ground. This was where my paternal grandfather had been laid to rest, right before I entered the academy. In contrast with my father's typically stern expression, my grandfather had always had a very kind and gentle face. Grandmother had also been a warm person, so honestly I had no idea how my father had turned out the way he did. Anyway, I digress.

Since becoming the acting governor, I'd found myself thinking about my late grandfather a great deal and coming to this little graveyard often. I believed he loved Armelia more than anyone else I'd ever known. I remembered him gazing fondly out the window at Armelia as I liked to do now, holding me and Berne up to take in the view and proudly telling us about the domain. He was such a gentle person that, for a time, I'd had no idea how he had survived as the prime minister in the capital, working amongst the snakes and foxes. I'd wondered that often, in the beginning.

It was different now; every time I came across a lasting effect my grandfather had made on Tasmeria's government, I came away impressed. I had to laugh at myself at the same time. I had been so foolish to think that I could take someone at face value and know immediately what kind of person they were. It seemed so obvious now, when I thought about it.

The grandfather I had known as a girl and the person he had been at work were two different people. On top of that, I had only known him when I was very young. He had been able to be precisely the person he wanted to be in front of me.

To the point, the only reason I was able to reform Armelia as completely as I was right now was because of the foundations my grandfather had laid. He had spent an enormous amount of time building Armelia's infrastructure. As such, I saw his legacy everywhere. The evidence was clear; he had left an astonishing trove of plans in case of future disasters—plans that stretched on into decades of work.

I had to admit that, while I had been so focused on progress and development, I'd forgotten many of the basics. It was incredibly impressive that Grandfather had accomplished everything he had while still serving as the prime minister. He had truly loved this land.

"I'm home," I said softly as I joined my hands in prayer. I silently apologized for bringing turmoil to Armelia, and I apologized further for bringing trouble to the family. Then I asked him to please watch over and protect me. Even though I knew he couldn't answer, I talked to him for a long time in this unspoken way.

"All right." I stood and turned. Tanya and Dida were waiting for me with smiles on their faces. "Let's go back home."

I began walking toward the house, my mind and heart feeling clearer and more at ease.

"I'd like more detailed information on what's in this report. Call in the person who prepared it."

Next, I indicated a towering stack of documents.

"I'm done checking these. Go ahead and deliver them where they belong."

Now I had to deal with the smaller mountain beside it. I almost felt like crying when I thought that this was the "only" thing I had left to do.

"These budgets need to be redone. Too many wasteful expenses. If that amount of money is truly necessary, I'll have to see more proof and a thorough explanation for the need."

I looked toward the neighboring stack. The same went for those papers. I was sure the departments who had sent them would be less than thrilled to redo them, but the finance division shared my opinion.

"The bridge mentioned in this document is definitely deteriorating. Go ahead and start the necessary repairs right away."

On the following day, I'd been cooped up in my study since morning. I was still surrounded by mountains of documents, but I was very slowly making my way through them. I wished I had more than one Iris to go around, but I silently chided myself for the thought—I needed to focus on work instead of entertaining frivolous wishes.

Each time I made a dent in the papers, Sebastian came in with another armload, so I truly wasn't making any progress.

Granted, if all the documents I had to check had been in the study all at once, I think it would have been too daunting to even contemplate.

Nevertheless, I felt my enthusiasm and motivation slowly chipping away. I knew I should have been grateful to Sebastian for bringing the documents in batches. He had a guilty look each time he came in, but it was no wonder so much work had piled up since I had been gone for so long.

On top of that, various projects we'd been in the middle of had suffered delays due to the church scandal and the time I'd spent in the capital. Many people in the government hadn't come to work while I'd been away, and they hadn't returned yet either. To put it simply, we were short-staffed, and it was becoming a serious problem. If it persisted any longer, the other Armelian officials would soon be under enormous pressure. More than anything, I didn't want to lose anyone to overwork, least of all those on the front lines who had remained loyal to me.

"We should be getting tax reports from all the regions soon, correct? We have to finish as many items on the agenda as we can before then..." I murmured.

As soon as Sebastian heard that, the expression on his face changed drastically—in a bad way, surprise, surprise.

Yes, yes, I know. I knew that adding more work to the mountains everyone was already buried under would be a tipping point. But the tax reports were vitally important. They would tell us every region's income and revenue, and we would use those numbers to predict the state of the duchy's economy going forward.

If we were fortunate enough to see substantial income growth, then we could run some expenditure estimates as well. On an individual level, high income tended to reflect in higher expenditures. Meanwhile, for businesses, it meant more capital to develop future endeavors. Having all this information in hand was crucial to predicting and manipulating the future of Armelia. Things were still rough out there, and I wanted to hurry up and get a move on.

The sound of a quill scratching on paper filled the room.

"My lady, please take a break," Tanya urged hesitantly.

Oh, I must've lost track of time, I thought as I glanced out the window. The sun was already setting. "Tanya? I've a favor to ask of you."

"Yes, my lady?"

"Could you make a list of all the officials who haven't reported to work since I was excommunicated? I want to see what they've been doing—and who's in their social circles."

"Of course."

"Then I'll take your advice and have a break. Go ahead and tell Sebastian to come here in a bit."

Tanya bowed her head and excused herself from the room. I took a sip of tea, savoring the sweetness of it as I relaxed. While I drank, I read through a letter I'd received from the marchioness of House Anderson. In other words, my uncle's wife.

House Armelia and House Anderson had been close for a long time, due to the intimate relationship between our grandfathers. They treated me extremely well and had been dearly concerned about me both after my expulsion and during my run-in with the Darryl Church.

House Anderson's domain bordered Armelia to the west, but because a range of treacherously steep mountains separated us, travelers either had to navigate around the entire range or reach them by sea. Honestly, we were both so busy that we simply couldn't visit each other often. Instead, we kept up with a steady stream of letters going both ways.

After I was done reading the letter, I decided I should probably get back to work. That was when Sebastian entered the room.

"I had a feeling you would resume your work, my lady."

"Perfect timing, Sebastian. There's something I want to ask you."

"What is it?"

"I'm sure you've already begun recruiting temporary workers for the merchant guild, haven't you?"

This initiative had been inspired by Dean, more or less. He had gotten his start there. The jobs weren't high responsibility or high status, but they involved tasks such as assisting with calculations and sorting through documents. We needed more staff members in order to process these tasks more quickly.

"Yes."

"And how is that going?"

"Not well, my lady. We're in the midst of the busy season right now, so we've had numerous applicants. However, some other establishments offer higher salaries, and it isn't as if we'll accept just anyone."

"I had a feeling." I sighed. "I have a suggestion, Sebastian."

"Yes?"

"Why not open up applications to the academy students attending the government track program?" I asked, and Sebastian's eyes widened at the proposal. "The job's responsibilities are all routine tasks. They can continue studying while they work. We'll be grateful for the extra help, and they can get experience in the field."

"Hm, that's ingenious. I'll contact the academy right away."

"Here, take this." I handed him a letter for the school. I figured I might as well use my status for all that it was worth—although I was sure that Headmaster Luka would think it an intriguing proposal and agree. "If the school says yes, may I entrust the negotiations to you?"

"Of course, my lady."

"All right, then. I'll leave you in charge of this matter."

"Very well, my lady."

I kept scratching my quill across the paper in the flickering lamplight. It felt like that was the only sound I'd been hearing lately.

"Mmm..." Once I finished writing, I set down my quill and stretched my arms up. The dreadfully unladylike sound of my stiff bones cracking and popping filled the room. Finally, I relaxed. I sank back into my chair, my arms falling limply over the armrests. It was terrible posture, of course, but I was alone, so it was permissible.

Slumped in my chair, I stared absently at the contents of the document I'd just written. Yes, that would do for the day. I realized with a wry chuckle that I hadn't set foot out of my study since I woke. I probably wouldn't even have stopped to eat had Tanya not told me to. I couldn't shake the tendency to become so absorbed in my work that I lost track of everything else around me. I had been like that in my previous life, but I'd been that way as Iris even before I regained the memories of that life. The habit was ingrained in my soul.

"Excuse me." There was a knock at the door and Tanya entered. "I saw the lights still on, so I thought maybe... And here you are, still working." She sighed, exasperated.

I laughed. She'd been different since we got home, but in a good way. Her rough edges had once again softened, and she wasn't as tense as she had been in the capital.

"Forgive me for meddling, but please go to bed," she urged. "I know I don't completely understand everything that you do, my lady, but if you collapse from overwork again, it will delay your plans even more."

Although, her concerns for me hadn't changed at all.

I laughed tiredly. "Yes, you're right. I was just thinking of calling it a night."

"I'm quite relieved."

"But first I'd like to hear your report. I was waiting here for you, thinking you'd be finished at any moment."

"I'm terribly sorry to have kept you waiting, my lady."

"I wanted to wait up for you. Your report, please."

She handed me a stack of documents, and as I read through them, she offered additional opinions that hadn't been recorded in writing.

"I see." Once I was done reading the report, I held the papers over the lamp and burned them. It would have been much more convenient if I had a fireplace, but since Armelia's climate was virtually perpetual springtime, we didn't have any.

At any rate, the documents were so sensitive that there was no way I could ever let anyone else lay eyes on them—especially not here, where I worked. I set the burning papers in a metal dish and waited until they were charred beyond recognition, and then I doused the flame with sand from a large bottle I kept on my desk for blotting.

"So they *have* been compromised..."

Tanya's report had revealed the names of those working in the Armelian government whose loyalties leaned more toward other domains over our own.

"It's a shame, but humans are fickle by nature, especially when they feel like things are unstable," said Tanya. "No matter how honest and upright your organization, there will always be those whose loyalty wavers."

"Yes, Tanya... Humans are fickle indeed. I know that all too well. But that's not the only issue, right? You can say it. It's easy for them to disrespect me because I'm a young woman."

"Well..."

"It's all right. It's true. I want you to gather all the people you noted in that report. Where shall we do it...? Oh, I know! How about the new church?"

"Very well, my lady. But...all of them?"

"Yes. Honestly, now that I've read your report, I've made up my mind about what to do with them. I'd like to meet them face-to-face first, though. All of them. Although I doubt they'll show."

"Very well."

"Oh, and Tanya? You did an incredible job, nailing down all those specific details. I think you're getting better and better at this."

"I do it all for you, my lady. And anyway, information is just information. It only becomes important after I bring it to you and you decide what is to be done with it."

She had a point; information in and of itself was nigh meaningless. One wrong step and it ended up baseless rumor, nothing more than a delusion. In this day and age, when you never knew what was true—or what could become untrue if the wrong person heard you knew—it was hard to trust anything.

"Tanya... What am I to you?"

"You are my stability, my lady. My pillar of support."

"I see. I know that you won't waver. I feel that deep inside of me, and that's why you serve as my eyes and ears. That's also why I'm able to trust the information you bring me and use it without hesitation."

"I'm incredibly honored to hear that."

"Well, I think it's time for bed. Will you straighten up in here for me?"

"Of course, my lady."

The new church was absolutely splendid. It was lavishly outfitted, expressing the power and influence of Armelia—or perhaps that was going too far, the man thought with a chuckle. This was his first visit. As to why he hadn't come before, well, that had everything to do with the reason for the church's construction. He, along with a few other like-minded individuals, had abandoned their jobs and voluntarily stayed at home in protest of Iris's decision to demolish the old church. Their opinion on the matter could best be described as righteous indignation.

They'd done so because they had truly believed they were in the right; after all, Iris had ordered the destruction of a church, which was the backbone of righteousness. Even after they heard this new church was being constructed, none of them had visited it because of their convictions—not even after Iris had been found innocent at the inquiry. In fact, their resistance grew after learning of her so-called innocence. It didn't matter to them. Nor did it change the contempt they had felt for her once she was named acting governor.

They hadn't been directly involved with the group who sullied her name following the old church's demolition, but they still disapproved of her.

The man knew that it was in poor taste to have abandoned the governor; as her employee, he should have remained by her side. He thought perhaps it might have been better to speak out against her publicly during her excommunication instead of just confining himself to his house. Even if doing so would have angered her, he should have spoken to her instead of deciding words wouldn't get through and that therefore there was no point.

In any case, it was too late now. That was why he had continued to stay at home. He was thinking it was time to tender his resignation, but at the same time, he wondered if it was even necessary at this point. That was when the invitation arrived—an invitation from the party in question, Iris Lana Armelia.

Although, it wasn't an invitation so much as it was a summons to appear, or so he had thought when he first read it. It made no mention of his recent behavior, but he was sure that was why she had asked to see him. He did have to wonder why their meeting was being held at the new church.

"You need to settle things." That was what he'd told himself before coming here today.

One by one, other people like him, those who had abandoned their posts, began to trickle into the church. The mood was heavy, and none of them spoke.

"Thank you so much for being here today." Suddenly, Iris entered as well, breaking the silence. She wore a serene smile as she looked around the room. "I see some people chose not to come, but I expected that. It's time to begin, so I'll go ahead and say what I've come to say."

Her voice echoed off the walls and ceilings of the chapel, reverberating inside the man's body.

"Every single one of you here neglected your duties as government officials of Armelia at the time of my excommunication. I called you here today to speak with you. But first, do any of you have anything to say to me?"

No one spoke.

"All right, then. I shall begin. What *is* a government official?" Iris's expression hadn't changed. She was still smiling. But that just made the pressure grow. "You, over there."

She seemed irritated that no one was speaking and called on one of them directly.

"A government official serves as an aide for the governor, performing any duties they are assigned in order to make the domain run smoothly." The man delivered a general response with a smug smile.

Iris frowned and turned to the person standing next to him. "Mm-hmm. And what about you?"

The woman was startled for a moment, having been put on the spot, and she stammered. "I-I agree with him."

"So then, going by your definition, during my excommunication, none of you were actually serving as government officials, no?" Iris asked with a chuckle, hiding her mouth with a folding fan. "Think about it. You defied me, your leader, and abandoned your duties without permission. If your job is solely to follow the governor's instructions, and you did the opposite of that, then you're clearly no longer needed."

She watched as the blood drained from their faces.

"Let me rephrase the question. Why did you abandon your duties during my excommunication and stay at home? I want your answer." Iris gestured toward the man, who had been watching this whole time.

He knew he couldn't avert his gaze, but the intensity of her attention made him desperately want to. "Forgive me for being presumptuous, but I would like to ask you the same question. What does a governor do?"

He *knew* he should give a bland and inoffensive answer, but instead, that impertinence tumbled out of his mouth. His boldness surprised even himself.

"I don't like it when people answer a question with a question," said Iris.

"Nevertheless, we need that answer from you," the man insisted. Perhaps he no longer cared what happened. It wasn't as if he had pride to protect, or anything else at all. He had lost all that the moment he abandoned his post, as Iris said. All he had now was a desperate sense of resignation.

"The job of a governor is one to take pride in. They protect the citizens, care for them, and enrich their lives. They must feel a deep sense of belonging with their domain in order to oversee the people."

"Precisely. And that's why I abandoned my duties."

Iris frowned, displeased. "You'll have to elaborate."

"Pardon me. I also believe that it's the job of the governor to protect and guide their citizens. That's why I abandoned my duties as an Armelian official following your excommunication. How can one guide citizens if they are accused of a crime by the church, which serves as the very foundation of our beliefs? Reformation is all well and good, but this incident caused the citizens to lose trust in those reforms as led by this governor— you. How can a governor inspire their citizens to dream if they are the one destroying dreams? That was what I thought, and that was the reason why I resisted you—why I abstained from work."

"You're awfully good at talking, aren't you?" Iris's words lit an indignant fire inside of him. Before he could object, she continued. "Are you sure it wasn't because you felt threatened having a young girl such as myself stand above you, giving you orders?"

Her response extinguished his anger. She had identified feelings within himself that he hadn't noticed—no, that he had *purposefully* avoided so as not to notice them. He couldn't deny her suggestion. He had opposed her appointment as acting governor from the very beginning.

Why, he had thought, would someone who had been scorned by the royal family and refused to learn from it be chosen as the acting governor?

At first, he'd thought it was just a whim on the part of the true governor, that Iris would just hold the title in name only. Then she started poking her nose into all governmental affairs. In the beginning, it only annoyed him, but once her plans in the duchy took off and he learned she had the backing of the queen dowager...he began to resent her very presence. Yet he suppressed those feelings. It wasn't until the excommunication that those feelings resurfaced and urged him to protest her by ignoring his job. However...

"I can't deny that I had those feelings. But the things I just said are *also* my true feelings."

"I see. Well? What do you feel a government official's job is?"

"To protect the livelihood of the citizens and aid the governor in any way in order to enrich their lives."

Iris let out a sigh.

Her reaction startled him slightly. He hesitantly lifted his gaze to look at her face. It was completely blank. Expressionless. Then in the next moment, a smile larger than she'd yet given spread across her face. Under normal circumstances, one might think such a smile on such fine features was beautiful. Instead, it was so incredibly fierce that he became intimidated.

"I see, I see. In that case, there's no need for you to look as if you're awaiting execution, then!"

The man hadn't realized he had such an expression until she said it.

"A government official is an *aide*. An *aide* to the *leader*. And an aide must never disobey their leader. More than that, thinking so little of the citizens is, in short, a crime. There's no need to feel ashamed if you took pride in defying me. But the scandal is over, so continuing to neglect your duties is delaying government progress, which in turn hurts the citizens. If a government official is supposed to serve the citizens, then you have failed, and you are guilty of a crime."

"But you were falsely charged, and—"

"Please. Don't pretend as if I have your sympathies, or as if you have any regrets for defying me. At this point, it would be nothing more than a nuisance. I've never once thought any of you were truly on my side, even from the beginning."

"Well...!" The man was deeply shocked to hear this.

"I'm not asking for personal loyalty, nor a sense of obligation, not from any of you. All I want is for you to do your jobs."

Iris's voice had taken on a quiet, lilting tone, but as she spoke, her words became stronger and stronger, like they were taking on a pulse of their own. "Do your jobs for the sake of the citizens. If you so strongly disapprove of me, then unite the public and overthrow me. You are no longer in a protected position. *Your* role is to protect. And you should take pride in that."

The man's heart felt hot, but it was a different fire burning inside him now. Was it excitement? Passion? He thought he could see the same heat rising from Iris—as if she were showing him a dream. How could such a small, delicate girl carry such an intense, searing flame within?

"Again, I won't ask for loyalty. But I will overlook this incident. Now hurry up and get back to work, all of you."

"You're forgiving us?" someone asked. The man looked over at them—didn't they understand that such a question was beside the point?

"It's not a matter of forgiveness, because I don't seek your favor. Therefore, your question is nothing. It doesn't matter if you acted out of loathing for me or whether you bent to the will of others—as long as you didn't betray Armelia or its citizens. I don't believe you did, so I am inviting you to return. Because if you don't..."

"If we don't?"

Iris's smile grew deeper. "There's no need for you to know. Or are you planning not to come back?"

No one answered.

"That's what I thought. Hurry up and get back to work. We don't have much time."

I stared absently at the vacant church once the crowd had gone.

"You were terribly stern," Tanya said. "It wasn't like you."

I smiled at her. "What would be like me?"

Tanya didn't answer right away. "My lady, forgive me for saying so, but I thought you were acting differently when we were in the capital. I felt like you were purposefully trying to make yourself out to be the villain."

I blinked at her in surprise. "Perhaps the scheming in the capital did change me. Or maybe it started when Dida asked me if I was prepared..."

His question had stripped away any naiveté I had left. I had been focused entirely on the future, chasing my ideals as I moved toward it.

Since regaining my past life's memories, I'd been guided by them—by all that time I'd spent as an ordinary office worker in a peaceful world. I had no intention of denying that.

At the same time, I'd felt like I was in a dream. Being faced with the surreal circumstances of my reincarnation had cloaked me in a strange reverie. I'd tried my best to ignore it, but Dida's question had shredded through the veil. It had forced me to see that I lived a real life.

As the acting governor of Armelia, I was responsible for the lives of its citizens in both the best and worst senses of the word. The moment I truly grasped that, I said farewell to the innocence of childhood, which had been filled with nothing but pure and beautiful things. Simultaneously, my past self said goodbye to her memories of a peaceful life.

I could no longer afford any weaknesses; my enemies would take any openings to eat me alive. Never again would I stand for being subjected to an incident like the excommunication or otherwise being falsely accused of a crime I had not committed.

"Don't worry," I said. "I know that if I make a mistake and step down the wrong path, the people I trust will stop me."

"Like Dida did?"

"Yes, exactly."

My people acted to carry out my orders, but when they thought I was truly wrong, they told me so. I knew I could trust them to speak up. For now, anyway. I could trust Sebastian, Dida, Lyle, Rehme, Sei, Merida, and Dean. Every one of them would pull me back if I ever strayed from the right path.

Although I did suspect that Tanya would give in to anything I said. But that was fine.

"May I ask you something else, my lady?"

I nodded my approval.

"Why did you arrange this meeting in the church, of all places?"

"Oh, that?" I laughed. "Because I thought it rather fitting."

Tanya gave me a puzzled look.

"This church symbolizes the entire scandal," I said. "It wouldn't be an exaggeration to say that it also represents the future of the Darryl Church."

Father Rafsimons had said as much himself.

Father Rafiel was giving free medical treatment to poor citizens at this very church. It also served as a home for Armelia's orphans. More and more volunteers from our capital were coming to help these endeavors. When he'd heard of it, Father Rafsimons had said this church was the very embodiment of Darryl's core values.

"I don't intend to hound the church, not aggressively. It wouldn't be worth it." I turned my gaze toward the altar. It felt like ages since I had stood there giving a speech after my excommunication. "I don't know if God truly exists. I do believe. But *that's* who I believe in—God, not the Darryl Church."

"My lady, that's..." Tanya's face turned pale. I had, to be fair, said something rather heretical.

"Tanya, have you forgotten what the church did? They were supposed to act as the agents of God, but instead, they falsely accused me, put me on trial, and interfered with the royal power struggle." I could hear the venom in my tone, even sharper than it had been in my head. "These so-called servants of God let their own personal greed and ambition usurp everything the church stood for. I suppose that sort of corruption is only natural for humans. And that is exactly why I won't place my trust in the church. I *can't*."

At this moment, I couldn't even bear to pray to God—not so long as there were people hiding behind Her name to further their selfishness.

"Remember what I said before? This is an expression of what I'm prepared to do. I have no intention of disavowing everything the church stands for. I know that we need faith to bring the citizens together. But this incident proved that the Darryl Church isn't, at its heart, a benevolent organization. They are a self-serving political body set on manipulating the throne. You must not believe their claim to stand for the people. And I will fight anything that fails to stand for the people. Thus, I will not pander to the Darryl Church, nor will I do as they say. I will treat them as if they are my opponent on the playing field. That is my decision. I hope they pay me the same respect. Regardless, I will protect the people not by relying on God or pandering to Her supposed servants, but by fighting for them with my own two hands."

I turned my gaze from Tanya back to the altar.

"I don't regret tearing down that old church, or the protest it inspired, or being decried for my actions. But I do regret something—my failure to predict that demolishing that structure would bring about such a catastrophe."

Tanya said, "I think it would have been difficult to predict such a thing. Didn't your father tell you as much himself?"

"Yes, I suppose you're right." I laughed softly.

Just then, the door opened, and some of the children who lived at the church tumbled in.

"Oh! It's Alice!"

"Hey, you're right! What are you doing here?"

"Come see Miss Mina with us!"

Their cheerful voices echoed throughout the church. The children clamored as they dashed over and surrounded me.

I knelt down to be eye level with them. "Okay. But she might be surprised if I show up so suddenly, so why don't you go tell her that I'm here first?"

"Will you really come, though?"

"Of course. I promise," I assured them with a smile.

The children seemed satisfied with this, and they ran back off toward the door.

As I watched them go, I said, "I have no real regrets, Tanya—because I helped protect their future."

"My lady..."

"You know what I was thinking? They're little Tanyas."

She gave me a puzzled look.

"They remind me of you when you were small. Your circumstances were far more terrible, granted. Even so, you were the only one I was permitted to take in at the time. Ever since, I've done my job because I want, more than anything, to protect children like you. So I couldn't possibly regret a thing."

"They seem so happy. They're very fortunate."

"Are you not happy, too, Tanya?"

"Of course I am. That's why I know they will be as well. Because they're little 'me's, right?"

I laughed out loud. I'd never thought I'd hear such words coming out of her mouth.

"I'm sure they're very impatient to see you, my lady. Shall we go?"

"Yes, let's," I agreed, and we both headed toward the door.

"Miss Mina!"

Four children scrambled into the kitchen where Mina was preparing dinner.

"Hey, now! It's dangerous in here," she scolded them. "You're supposed to ask me before you come inside, remember?"

"We're sorry..."

The four of them hung their heads, which drew a wry smile from Mina. She put down her knife and crouched to look them directly in the eyes. "Well? What is it?"

"Alice is here!"

"Oh, my!" Mina exclaimed with surprise; she was so startled that the children seemed bewildered by her reaction. "I can't believe the gove—I mean, Lady Alice is here! What to do?!"

"Children, I thought I told you not to go into the chapel." Father Rafiel had been taking a break and walked into the kitchen, having heard the commotion.

"Father Rafiel," Mina gasped. "Lady Ir—I mean, Lady Alice is here!"

"I'm aware. She asked to use the chapel for a meeting. Did she not mention it to you?"

"No!" Mina glared at Father Rafiel, who wore his usual serene smile. "I-I must prepare some tea right away! Ah, but first I should go greet her, and—"

"Calm down, Mina."

"Excuse us." Tanya called out at the same time. Therefore, Mina didn't hear what Father Rafiel said—she had bolted toward the front door in a panic.

Father Rafiel chuckled and followed after her.

"W-welcome, Lady Ir—ah! Lady Alice! And Tanya."

Even though there wasn't a profound distance from the kitchen to the front door, Mina had sprinted at full speed. She was panting, both because she was out of breath and because she was so nervous. But when she saw Iris, she had to do a double take.

"No need to be so formal, Mina. And thank you so much for answering my sudden request to use the space for today, Father Rafiel."

Iris greeted them both, pulling Mina back to herself.

"Not at all. I'm glad I could be of some help," Father Rafiel said with a smile. "By the way, Lady Alice, forgive me for being so frank, but are you feeling quite well?"

Mina nodded in agreement from his side. This was the reason she had been so startled when she laid eyes on Iris. The governor looked much thinner than Mina remembered—and she was so pale that her skin was nearly translucent.

Iris smiled awkwardly as they gave her concerned looks. "I've been extremely busy with work. But thanks to you, I've finally caught up with a rather important matter."

"Oh, I'm so glad to hear that! Was there something in particular you needed from us?"

"No, I just wanted to say hello. And to come see my friends, of course."

"Your friends...?"

"Yes! Right, everyone?" Iris smiled and glanced behind Mina and Father Rafiel. She met eyes with the grinning children who had just appeared.

"Alice is here! Why'd you come today?"

"Guess what, Alice? I can read now!"

"Will you play with me today, Alice? You promised last time!"

Mina was powerless to stop the children, who eagerly crowded around Iris. Fortunately, Iris wasn't at all bothered by the attention; in fact, she smiled at them happily.

"That's right, I did promise!" she laughed. "Father Rafiel, Mina, I'm so sorry for coming over unannounced. Do you mind if I play with the children?"

"Oh, my, not at all! As long as they're not troubling you!" Mina said. "Please come in."

"Thank you." Iris smiled down at the children. "Why don't we do something new today and read to each other?"

There was a chorus of cheers as the children tugged on her hands and pulled her inside. Mina now knew Iris's true identity, which made the scene beyond anxiety-inducing for her.

Meanwhile, Father Rafiel continued to smile warmly. "Mina, I know you respect her, but please try not to be so obvious in front of the children. They're terribly clever, you know."

"Yes..." Mina's response was so half-hearted that the unspoken *That's impossible...* was nearly audible. Father Rafiel had to chuckle as they rejoined the group.

By the time they were back inside, the children had already started playing with Iris.

"What are they doing?" Father Rafiel asked Tanya with interest as he watched.

"Apparently, the game is called Constables and Robbers." Tanya proceeded to explain the rules to the priest, who listened with genuine curiosity.

"That sounds interesting indeed. I've never heard of it before. Did she come up with the game?"

"I'm not sure."

Neither of them looked at each other as they spoke. They were both too absorbed in fondly watching Iris and the children. For her part, Mina seemed lost in thought.

"Why is Lady Iris so..." she murmured quietly to herself.

Tanya tensed at hearing her mistress's name. "What about Lady Iris?" she asked sternly.

"Pardon me. I was just wondering how Lady Iris could be so very kind."

Tanya's eyes widened.

Mina laughed briefly at this, but then a sad expression came over her face. "We got her involved in so much trouble, but she hasn't blamed us, not once. And here she is, coming over to visit."

"Mina..." Father Rafiel looked at her with concern.

"When I think of how much Lady Alice endured during her excommunication—oh, we're to blame for it! We...no, I—I should have been more aware of what was going on. Then she never would have had to suffer so. But we let her get involved and placed such a heavy burden on her. Yet she still treats us just as she ever did. We've nothing to offer, and she protects us. It's just so sad to me. I'm frustrated." By the end, Mina's voice was trembling.

"Mina, it isn't your fault," said Father Rafiel. "If I hadn't been so stubborn—if I'd come back to everyone sooner, perhaps I could have changed something."

Father Rafiel's words didn't seem to help, because Mina only looked more depressed.

Tanya, however, did not indulge the mood. "That's just how Lady Alice is."

She didn't elaborate. She didn't have to either. They could see by the look on her face just how proud she was of her mistress.

"That was so fun! Would you mind if I take a little break?"

Iris's voice interrupted their discussion, and no sooner were the words out of her mouth than Tanya rushed to her mistress's side. She pulled out a handkerchief and began to dab the sweat off of Iris's forehead and neck.

"Lady Alice..." Mina murmured.

"Yes, Mina? Oh, you look so stressed. Is something the matter?" Iris's gaze flicked over to Father Rafiel questioningly.

An apologetic look came over his face, and he shook his head.

Mina piped up as well, shaking her head. "N-no, of course not! Everything here is so wonderful!"

"I'm glad to hear that," said Iris. "But please don't hesitate to let me know if you ever need anything."

Once again, Mina thought, *How can she be so genuinely kind?*

She felt like she might burst into tears. What *was* she feeling? Sadness? Pity? No, it wasn't exactly either of those things.

She couldn't put her finger on it, but that unnamed emotion rose up from deep within her.

"Thank you for being so considerate," Mina said sincerely. "Although, um, Lady Alice? May I ask you something?"

"What is it?"

"Do you ever go out on the town?"

"Why do you ask?"

"I've been a bit worried. No one's seen you lately."

Iris smiled sheepishly. "I can't show my face in public like I used to. It's far more difficult to walk through town from a security standpoint as well."

Mina's shoulders slumped. As they did, Iris's expression grew even more sheepish.

"That's the official answer, of course," Iris said. "But there's no problematic reason, I promise. To be honest with you...I think I may just be scared, that's all."

"Scared?"

"Yes. Of how the people in town will react to me. It's only natural that they'll treat me differently now that they know my true identity. I understand that. But I caused a lot of trouble for everyone with this excommunication business. I'm relieved there were no riots, but I'm sure if I were to show my face, the people would have a great deal to say to me. To be honest, I'm so frightened of what they might say that I simply can't go out like I used to." Iris laughed as if it were all a joke. "A pathetic excuse for a governor, am I not? Please forget I said anything."

Mina didn't laugh in kind. In fact, the light had disappeared from her eyes. At the same time, she had an epiphany. She now understood what feeling was welling within her—despair. Grief at her lack of power. It weighed so heavily on her that it was physically painful. The urge to do something for Iris burned in her chest.

"Lady Alice...forgive me for my impudence, but..." Mina's voice trembled. It was all she could do not to scream. "Please don't take me—or any of us—for fools!"

In the end, her emotions were so uncontrollable that they broke the dam. Despite all her good sense, her feelings spilled out.

For a split second, Father Rafiel's face was pure shock, but he said nothing. It seemed he had decided to let Mina say her piece.

"I know that from your standpoint, we seem weak," said Mina. "We live in small, closed worlds, and we can't possibly know everything our leaders are up to. It's all we can do to keep up with our own little lives."

The people went to work every day, came home, and ate. Then they fell asleep, woke, and started the process all over again, praying that the new day would be as peaceful as the previous.

They prayed because they understood they had to be grateful for that peace. They knew themselves blessed if they didn't have to worry about where their next meal was coming from, and if they had a job from which they received worthy pay. The average citizen didn't understand the minutiae of how governmental policies actually shaped their daily lives. They either thought it above their heads or gave up trying to understand because they thought something like: *Even if I understood, it's not like I could change anything, so what's the point?*

To them, the royal family and the nobility lived in an entirely different world. The only time these high-born individuals entered into their thoughts was when they heard particularly interesting rumors and the like. In short, that was usually a sign that the government was moving in a bad direction.

When jobs were scarce, no one had money, and the price of food at the market went up, the air in town became heavy, and the people grew dour and gloomy. Mina knew this all too well; she had lived in another domain before she was taken in by the nun who'd run the old orphanage. She remembered that, at such times, the people spoke out against those above them. That angered the authorities and drove them to further oppress the citizens, which in turn made the people even more rebellious. Such circumstances made the air grow even heavier.

To be sure, Iris's excommunication had caused a stir—and yes, some people here and there still criticized her. But...

"Even so, we're *not* fools," Mina declared. "We understand how much you've done for Armelia!"

So many people had come out in support of Iris.

"Life is so much easier than it was before!"

"Our new governor really cares about us."

"There must be some kind of mistake!"

Mina didn't know all of what Iris had or hadn't done, but everything she'd done in the duchy had made life easier for its people and brought smiles back to their faces.

There were more doctors to treat the sick, and with the increase in literacy, the people were better protected from traveling merchants looking to swindle them. Farmers who lived in the regions with poor soil had been given access to education and new means to make a living. The children of Armelia smiled because they could dream of their futures.

Every day, so many people spoke of Iris. They weren't spreading gossip to entertain themselves—they shared exciting rumors they'd heard of her work and deeds, and they did so with smiles on their faces.

"We *are* weak," Mina acknowledged. "But I won't stand for anyone using our weakness to blame you for anything."

Mina knew what it meant to be a woman, just as Iris did. Mina was slightly older, but they were of the same generation. Being a woman meant people thinking certain things about you. It didn't matter that Mina and Iris were on completely different ends of the power spectrum—Iris had influence, strength, wealth, none of which Mina possessed.

But Iris was human, just like anyone else. Mina understood that well, what with all the time she'd spent with her. Iris wasn't some intangible idea. She was a real, live, breathing person—one who stood before Mina at this very moment, so overworked that she was wasting away before her eyes. Mina couldn't let her get away with this any longer.

If she did, it would just give those who already hated working women even more ammunition.

"Please, Lady Alice. Please don't blame yourself anymore. I can't forgive anyone who criticizes you, even if that person is you."

Iris's eyes widened, and then tears began to stream down her face. Her reaction shocked Mina.

"Ah! You made Alice cry, Miss Mina!"

"That's not nice!"

The children chided Mina as Iris sniffled.

Iris shook her head, wiping the tears away. "No, children, it's fine. I'm actually very happy."

"You cry when you're happy?"

"That's right. Tears can come out of your eyes when you're happy, too. And Miss Mina said something so sweet that all these happy tears are coming out of my eyes."

The children breathed a sigh of relief, as did Mina.

"Alice, Mina, perhaps you'd each like a cool cloth for your faces?" Tanya asked.

Mina nodded through her own tears. "Ah, yes. Tanya, in here." And she led the way into the kitchen.

After Tanya retrieved dampened handkerchiefs for both women, Father Rafiel and Iris sat across from each other.

Mina had taken the children to put them down for their naps. Although they usually brimmed with energy, many were already worn out from their busy day of running around with Iris.

"I'm so sorry about today, what with the children demanding your attention, and then the thing with Mina..." Father Rafiel trailed off.

"Not all. I love playing with the children. You needn't apologize. As for Mina's words...I'm sorry you had to see me in such a state. I really did appreciate what she said. I suppose I'll have to figure out a new disguise so I can go back to town incognito."

Father Rafiel looked troubled. "You truly are so kind to others and so hard on yourself."

"You think so? You know what happened in the chapel earlier, don't you?" Iris asked.

Father Rafiel smiled tightly, but he didn't chide her. Rather, he looked as though he had expected this. "Being kind to people is different from indulging them when they've done something wrong."

Iris laughed. "I suppose you're right. Now what's our friend up to these days?"

"Serving with his peers. I think his time at the academy left him rather naive to a number of things," Father Rafiel said with a new sort of smile.

Iris smiled back at him. "I'm relieved to have you watching over him. And I'm sorry for asking you to do this."

"Not at all. I owe you an incredible debt, after all."

"I see... Tangentially, I heard you've seen Noryu?"

Father Rafiel gave her a look of surprise. "You're well informed, my lady."

Noryu was a priest who had carried out the orders of the former pope during Iris's excommunication. He was currently awaiting trial for his involvement, and he had been jailed in the capital until a verdict could be reached.

"He told me it was all your fault," Father Rafiel said with a laugh. "However, I had removed myself from the power struggle in the capital of my own volition. It would have always been difficult to get the promotion he wanted while working under me. I suspect his resentment boiled up."

"It feels strange to hear about clergymen yearning for promotions."

"I suppose it does." Father Rafiel laughed again. "Humans are difficult creatures. They all have different ways of thinking. You could gather ten people in a room, ask for their opinion on any given thing, and they'd all have something different to say. Even if they all believe in God, they all have their own interpretation of the same divine doctrines. I encourage you to ask a group yourself sometime. It's quite fascinating."

"I'll keep that in mind."

"To the point... Those different opinions can come from different values. Noryu and I certainly differed in our values, but as we never discussed the difference in our opinions, we had no opportunity to express that difference. Consequently, his emotions became pent up, and the explosion was inevitable. This was a mistake on my part, one that ended up causing you no end of trouble. I'm terribly sorry."

"Please, don't be. Noryu is ultimately responsible for his own actions. But hearing your take is truly helpful. You're right; as the one responsible for this domain, I need to consider listening to my people far more than I have."

"I think you already listen to them. Then again, our positions have always been quite different. I suppose I didn't expect that my words would actually be of service..."

"But you see, my position is the reason I should take my people's voices seriously. If I don't hear their opinions, I'll end up forcing my own onto them. Even if I'm just trying to help, if I don't really listen, their resentments will build up as well. I want to make sure that doesn't happen."

Father Rafiel looked thoughtful. "It's funny...you act nothing like the rest of the nobility, yet you're more noble than any I've ever met."

Iris laughed. "I'm a contradiction, then? How would you describe me?"

"I've gone so long watching aristocrats serve themselves first and none after. You're not like that. You truly love your people, and they truly love you in turn. Which is to say: It's important to listen to people, but I'm sure that if you tell them how you feel, they'll trust you. And they'll follow you, no matter what."

"How I feel..." A thoughtful look came over Iris's face.

"Pardon me for speaking out of turn."

"No, not at all. It brings me satisfaction to hear you speak honestly. Although I really should be going now."

"Of course. Please come back again soon."

Father Rafiel showed Iris to the front door, and Mina joined them along the way.

After Iris departed, Mina spoke in a quiet voice. "She's an aristocrat, isn't she? The sort of person a regular citizen like me dares not speak to... The daughter of a duke. Completely out of my reach, right?"

It sounded more like she was asking herself rather than Father Rafiel.

"So why is she so kind to us? Why is she always so concerned?" Once again, tears sprang to Mina's eyes. "The old lady who owns the florist shop, the old man who runs the restaurant on the corner—all the people I see in town—they're always talking about Lady Iris. Everyone here is unbearably fond of 'Alice.'"

"They are."

"So when she told us why she no longer comes to town—I cursed my own helplessness. I wondered what I could do, but I realized there was nothing." Mina clenched her fists. "But no matter how much I hate my helplessness, I can't hide behind it. I think everyone who knows Lady Iris feels the same way—not even just them. The people who knew what was happening to the orphans and regret not helping them, they probably feel it, too. There are so many people she's helped who we don't even know. So many lives she's touched both as Lady Iris and Lady Alice."

"I'm sure she'll start coming around again. She said she was going to get a new disguise."

Mina burst into tears. "I'm glad to hear that." But through the tears, a broad smile had spread over her face. "I'm sure everyone will be so happy."

"I'm sure you're right." Father Rafiel smiled back at her.

On the second floor of a completely ordinary shop stood a woman. Yuri. She wasn't wearing one of her usual pretty dresses. Instead, she was clad in a plain frock, the sort you'd see on any girl in any town.

"Divan, why must you always sneak up on me so quietly?" she asked, annoyed.

The man approaching her from behind laughed. "Well, well. I'm terribly sorry about that. I'm afraid it's just how I operate, so the young lady must forgive me."

Yuri frowned. "Hearing you speak so politely gives me the creeps."

"'Tis only fitting to speak in such a manner to an individual of most esteemed status, my lady. I really have to hand it to you. The prince's fiancée? Brilliant."

Yuri nodded stiffly. "You have my gratitude. You have protected me all this time, and you've always given me the information I needed. So, I always listen to you, and so, I'm here now. Well? What is it this time?"

"Oh, I just thought we could chat a bit."

"Chat?"

"Indeed. You know the dress of Armelian silk that you were so fond of? A very small number of them have reached stores in the capital."

"Oh, my. Yes, that dress was exquisite—I do want one."

"I thought as much." Divan's look was inscrutable. "You should ask the prince. I'm sure he would procure one for you."

"Do you think so, Divan? I think you're right." Yuri giggled, and her irritation dissipated as she smiled.

"Although it would be risky to do so. The prime minister's domain has already amassed great wealth, and that purchase would put even more money in his pockets."

"I suppose so. But Divan...isn't that your fault?"

"I beg your pardon?"

"Well, because of your blunder, that girl is still a member of high society. Even after I went through the trouble of introducing you to the pope and everything. But you flubbed that, and now she's grown even stronger."

"Yes, that was all due to my ineptitude," he agreed. "I sincerely apologize that things ended up the way they did despite your efforts."

"Honestly. Don't make the same mistake twice."

"Very well." Divan eyed Yuri thoughtfully. "You really despise her, don't you?"

"I do. I *hate* her. She was born with a silver spoon in her mouth, and she acts like she was entitled to it. People like her—I can't stand them. I thought for sure I would get to see her fall from grace once she was expelled from the academy, but..." Yuri paused and peered out the window, almost as if she were looking for Iris. "When I was trapped in that little town, I just kept thinking... that wasn't where I belonged. That someone as beautiful as me didn't deserve to wither away in a filthy place like that. That's why I worked so hard, and why I'll continue to do everything I must."

"You're so determined."

"I'm going to hold this country in the palm of my hand. I swear it. And I can't wait..." Yuri's voice cracked with excitement.

Divan had to applaud her.

"Oh, right, Divan, I did just as you said and pushed Van aside. He's disappeared now... Are you sure that was the right decision?"

"Yes, yes. It was. He would have remained useless if you'd kept him around, in any case. Now that you've turned him away, he'll be useful for the first time in his life."

"Hmm. I can't wait."

"It will be worth it." Divan smiled. "Relatedly, how is the prince doing?"

"Oh, he's wonderful," Yuri smiled as well. "Ahh, I'm a bit embarrassed to talk about him! But's he's just so adorable."

"Oh, my. Should I be worried that you're turning into your mother?"

Yuri's mood instantly changed, and the air between them iced over. Her face was expressionless, but her eyes shone sharply. "I'm nothing like my mother. And I won't ever be."

Divan remained unflappable and laughed. "Pleased to hear that. Well, then, until we meet again."

"Yes...until then."

"Rudy, I'm done," Alfred announced as he threw down his quill.

Rudius gave him a soft smile. "Well done, Your Highness. I'll take these where they need to go."

"Thanks." Alfred let out a sigh that had been building up

inside him. Now that he'd taken care of all the business at the palace, he could go to Armelia with a clear conscience.

"It should be fine if you take a longer stay," said Rudius. Alfred had said nothing aloud, but Rudius had a way of responding to his friend's thoughts.

Alfred gave him a crooked smile. "Yes, I think it should be fine. I've done more than enough. Although, I do wonder how we got into this position in the first place. What in the world were those officials thinking?"

"It seems they're extremely short-staffed at the castle."

The situation had deteriorated to the point that they no longer just needed spies in other countries and domains, but also in the castle itself. They were playing their game of musical chairs with the other royals, and everyone below them was fighting for power and position.

At this point, open attacks were expected at every level, but those required leveraging personal connections and bribes—and those who made serious plays kept on making fools of themselves. As a result, the truly gifted players never made a move in public, or even attempted to leave the field of play entirely. Alfred had picked up as many of those as he could and added them to his own team.

"Armelia's workforce is also suffering, but I envy them all the same. They genuinely don't have enough people. It's worse when you have people but they're simply unproductive."

All of this back and forth in the power struggle had done horrors to the kingdom's productivity. Alfred wasn't sure how many actual public servants were even left.

"I'm going to rest for a bit. Wake me in an hour," Alfred told Rudius with a heavy sigh.

"If you're going to rest, why not go to your bedroom?"

"I'm fine here."

"Very well."

After Rudius left, Alfred let out yet another sigh and closed his eyes. Perhaps it was the exhaustion, but lately, he'd found himself thinking of his past. Memories from his boyhood. Most of them weren't particularly good.

The first thing he remembered was being surrounded by adults. As the first-born prince, he was taken from his parents immediately after his birth and reared by caretakers.

He was a cold child. At the same time, he proved clever. From the age of about three, he became cautious of people and the motives with which they approached him. He observed the adults around him with great care, studying them to learn who meant what they said and who didn't. Envy, greed, vanity, arrogance, wrath, sloth...he learned what triggered every sin, how they manifested, and what reactions they invited.

(He'd told Rudius of his childhood thoughts once, and Rudius had smiled, exasperated. "I never imagined a three-year-old would think such things, Your Highness.")

Then Prince Edward was born, complicating Alfred's life even more. Ellia, who at the time was just the king's mistress, gained even more power at court and more people flocked to her side.

Alfred's mother, Queen Sharia, was humiliated and more or less lost her status.

Alfred's memories of her were hazy, to say the least. He never had much occasion to interact with her, though that might have changed, if she hadn't died when he was so very young. Those who had known her told him that she had been frail but gentle, and she had despised fighting. Alfred thought a person like that must have felt terribly out of place in the cutthroat world of the court.

Yet she had endured. Being sickly, she could have withdrawn to the palace as the queen dowager had. Perhaps it was more accurate to say that she remained despite herself. The king had been too attached to let her go.

"Why are you here?" Alfred asked her once. "You don't belong in a place like this." He said it from a place of concern. Seeing her treated so poorly day in and day out, he wanted to give her heart some ease.

Queen Sharia just smiled softly at him. "I love your father. That's why."

Alfred wanted to laugh and say, "I don't get it." He couldn't bring himself to; he respected his mother too much. He understood the king's love was all she had left. She believed in that intangible thing, and it kept her from running away. It held her to this dreadful place.

This amazed Alfred, not because he thought it was correct or clever, but because he saw such strength in his mother. At the same time, he had a powerful desire to blame the king for all the hardship his mother suffered.

The king was a person, but he was also an institution, a symbol and a tool who needed to represent the entire country. As such, he couldn't always do as he pleased, even when it came to protecting his beloved Queen Sharia from the ire of Ellia.

Perhaps he should have devoted himself solely to the system from the start. He had put his personal feelings first when he made Sharia his queen. All the horrors that had come with that position weren't her fault at all, Alfred thought.

If only the king had never set eyes on her. Then she could have fallen in love with anyone else and lived a peaceful life. She wouldn't have had her heart broken or been exposed to constant danger. She would never have worn that sad smile.

Queen Sharia grew even weaker after Leticia's birth, but the king only grew more attached to her. Of course, Ellia was unamused. Thus, she took action: to kill Queen Sharia.

Ellia had already gained control of the inner palace and those who worked there. No one had to tell Queen Sharia for her to realize as much. That was why she had told Alfred, "Protect Leticia."

She didn't say this to the king—she said it only to her son. Perhaps she had realized by then that the king was nothing but a tool in the hands of others. She had certainly realized that, at times, one must put one's interests ahead of one's relationships.

Alfred, wanting to keep his promise to his mother, acted immediately. He asked Rudius to help him see the queen dowager.

Until that meeting, under the watchful eye of Marquis Anderson, he made sure that only people who could be completely trusted were ever allowed near the young princess.

Finally, the day came. Alfred sneaked out of the castle to meet his grandmother, the queen dowager, for the first time. He begged her to take care of Leticia, offering his own freedom as collateral.

From the moment he met her, Alfred could tell that the queen dowager was deeply concerned for Queen Sharia, as well as for her two children. At the same time, the queen dowager proved she had once been a ruler by demonstrating her cunning and forethought.

So long as Alfred remained in the castle, she said, the fight over succession would only grow further inflamed. She was additionally afraid that Alfred, being so young, would be swept up in the power struggle as a puppet, not a person. She warned him then and there that even if she took him under her protection, they would only be delaying the inevitable conflict. So long as Alfred had royal blood flowing through his veins, he would always be the first prince, and for that, Ellia would always be out to kill him.

"So," said the queen dowager, "you must become more powerful. Learn to judge people so you won't be used. Forge a shield with which to protect yourself. A king is the quintessential symbol of power—so he mustn't let himself be taken advantage of. To hungry aristocrats, kings are like delicious nectar. If he shows the least sign of weakness, they'll eat him alive, no matter how they wound the kingdom when they do."

That was why the queen dowager wanted to avoid letting Edward become a prince. If he did, those ravenous aristocrats would gain a dangerous amount of power over the line of succession. Once they had that, the royal castle would begin to rot from the inside out.

The queen dowager heaved a troubled sigh. This succession crisis had become a deep abiding worry for her. "That is why you must gain your own power. And as you do, you must keep House Marea from matching your influence. That is my condition."

Alfred didn't even have to think about it. After all, power was what would keep him safe. Nevertheless, he realized it would be risky to gain influence too publicly. He couldn't pretend to be an idiot, either, or he risked getting dismissed from court. At least for now, under the queen dowager's protection, he could guarantee his safety for at least a few years and devote himself to his studies.

When he told the queen dowager his decision, she smiled. She seemed truly happy. "I'm quite strict!" she warned him.

"I'll do my best to make you proud," he said.

She laughed. He'd meant it in a stubborn way, but she didn't seem to mind. "You're a clever boy. I like you. Now become the type of boy I would regret ever letting go!"

Alfred had, by some means, just solidified her affection for him. She seemed almost ready to insist he remain by her side for the rest of his days.

"But take it easy on my old bones!" she said with a laugh.

Deep down, Alfred was frustrated by the state of things. By all rights, the first prince was the crown prince, expected to succeed the throne. But the queen dowager was right that if he didn't grow powerful enough to even step into the ring when he was older, he should make peace with losing his rights. Even if he did manage to end up on the throne, he would inherit a kingdom at war with itself.

If that happened, he had no doubt that the queen dowager would use her influence to remove him from power and back the second prince. She would use the fact that she had overthrown the first prince to win allies from the second prince's faction, and then once she had gotten close enough, would take control from them. She would use Edward as her puppet to establish the power she wanted.

"Yes, Grandmother," said Alfred, all this on his mind. "I'll do my best to remain in your favor."

After this meeting, Princess Leticia was quietly removed to the palace, along with Alfred.

Days after they left, Queen Sharia was killed. Her doctor claimed that Ellia was responsible. She had been poisoned, he said. Yet he was powerless.

Even though the physician knew that Ellia had been behind the murder of Alfred's mother, he had no influence to undo the cover up. And even if he'd said something, everyone who could have done anything was under Ellia's thumb.

It was all Alfred and the queen dowager could do to protect Leticia. For the first time in Alfred's life, he was left feeling bereft by his own helplessness.

Queen Sharia's funeral was modest and small. After the event, the king was so distressed that he became visibly haggard. Seeing his father in such a state made Alfred feel nothing.

Worse, the incident made Alfred the primary target of Ellia's ire. She had truly believed that the king's heart would belong only to her once Queen Sharia was dead. But once it was clear that this would not happen and her dreams were shattered, Ellia cracked as well. She took on the role of a tragic woman scorned by the love she most desired.

Alfred never felt the least bit of pity for her. In truth, he was glad that he was able to see her actions so clearly.

One day, the king summoned Alfred to him and said, "My beloved wife bore me a daughter."

Alfred's first reaction was anger; after all this time, *now* the king asked after Leticia? He'd never cared a whit about the children when their mother was alive, that was for sure.

"I'm sure she's a beautiful girl. She must look just like her mother. I wish to see her."

The instant Alfred heard that, his irritation vanished. Instead, a chill ran down his spine. He knew instantly that this was dangerous. Leticia looked so much like their mother that the king would without a doubt instantly adore her. He would try to fill the hole in his heart left by his late wife by showering his daughter with affection. And that would make Ellia target Leticia.

Ellia already felt jilted. There was no telling what she might do if she saw the king dote on Leticia. The fact that his blood flowed through the princess's veins wouldn't even register in her jealousy-addled mind.

"The queen dowager sees to Leticia's care," said Alfred, choosing his words carefully. "She always says that my sister is the spitting image of you, Father."

At this, the king lost interest in Leticia. He never again asked to see her.

Although it seemed things in the castle were peaceful again, Queen Ellia continued to target Alfred's life and began dispatching assassins. He had no time to waste when it came to training to win this battle. As such, his skills progressed so rapidly that they left General Gazell tongue-tied. Alfred was so stubborn about his training that he made lasting connections during it. The general put him through hell—but only out of adoration. Alfred was truly grateful for it.

Meanwhile, being trapped in the gilded cage of the palace gave Alfred a hunger for knowledge. Within a few years, his existence had been largely forgotten, and he started to be more forward about going out.

Alfred sneaked into the castle and pretended to be a diplomat. He infiltrated the barracks and trained alongside the soldiers. He traveled to other domains and observed life there. Along the way, he recruited any particularly skilled people he met to his service. At last, he changed his name and attended the academy, then joined the merchant guild. By that time, the queen dowager no longer objected to his forays into the public eye. In fact, she seemed to take pleasure in it.

At last, Alfred's thoughts turned to the day he'd met Iris at the palace. He wondered if she remembered.

She probably doesn't, he thought with an inward chuckle. They had both been very young at the time, after all.

Iris's mother, Merellis, had brought her to the palace for a visit, and the children had run into each other in the gardens.

"Who are you?" Iris had asked him, her large eyes sparkling with curiosity.

That had been the beginning of it all. Iris assumed Alfred was a live-in apprentice servant who worked at the palace, and they saw each other constantly after that. He came to look forward to their meetings. Most of the time, it had just been her talking away animatedly with her eyes shining as he nodded and listened.

Then, one day, she said, "I can't come here anymore."

"Why?"

"I have to start learning how to become a member of the royal family. So I'll have to be at home all the time."

"Do you mean...you're marrying into the royal family?" Alfred asked tentatively. "You're engaged to the second prince?"

"Ah! That's exactly how Grandmother reacted! Prince Ed is such a lovely person, though."

"Oh? And what makes you think that?"

"Well, I was at his birthday party. Everyone always says I'm cute, but you know, they only say that because when they look at me, they see my mother's face. They think I'll turn out just like her. The people who don't think that say I look like my father. I think that either way, people are more attracted to my family's power than to my appearance. When I told Prince Ed that, he laughed. He said, 'I wouldn't be happy if someone said I was cute, especially not if they're just comparing me to my family.' Then he said, 'Make those people who compare you to your parents eat their words. You're your own person, and you should feel confident.' Don't you think he's the loveliest person?"

"Yeah..."

"That's when I thought, 'Oh, I want to stand by his side!' My parents and grandmother were totally against it, though. But I begged and begged, and they finally agreed. In exchange, I have to go back to the duchy with Mother and study at our estate. I have to be able to protect Prince Ed from all the bad people."

"Oh..."

"I'm going to try really hard so I can be with him. But I won't be able to see Grandmother Iria anymore, or my father. Or you. I'm really sad." Fat tears streamed down Iris's cheeks.

Alfred smiled. He felt like crying too—because hearing of Iris's betrothal to the second prince only spelled danger for him.

"It's not like you're going away forever. If you want to see someone, you can see them. If you really want to, you'll find a way," he murmured as he wiped her tears away. "Study very hard to protect the second prince so that the bad grown-ups don't take advantage of him. Make him love you so much that he'd choose you over his own family. If you do that, your hard work will be worth it."

Alfred could only hope that Iris would be able to keep the second prince away from House Marea.

It was a gamble on his part. Honestly, all he wanted to do was thwart Iris's engagement to the second prince. But he couldn't. First of all, he didn't have the power to interfere with a decision the prime minister and the queen dowager had jointly made. Secondly, Iris was around the same age as Leticia. Her cheeks were flushed pink, her big eyes filled with determination. Just looking at her made Alfred feel close to her, for some reason.

"Never fear. There's nothing to worry about. I know you can do it." Alfred rested his forehead against hers. "I do this for my little sister to make her feel better."

After that, he didn't see Iris again until they passed each other in the halls of the academy. He wondered if she had been working hard. In truth, he was disappointed when he saw her again—though he couldn't put his finger on what it was about her that disappointed him, or what he had been hoping for.

Only when he saw her again, working as the acting governor, did he realize that he had been wrong. In fact, he praised his childhood self for the hunch he'd had all those years ago.

Maybe he'd just been blinded by jealousy when he heard rumors about her at the academy...

In any case, the queen dowager had felt proud relief when she saw how Iris had grown at the Foundation Day party. Simultaneously, Alfred's world began to take on new color.

In their bloodthirsty world, where everyone wore a fake smile, Iris still possessed the innocent smile of a young girl. But she also grew angry at the absurdity of the world, and she agonized over her own powerlessness. Alfred had thought she would show her feelings as freely as she had when she was young, but instead she mastered her emotions and gritted her teeth. She pushed herself forward, coming up with new ideas and chasing victory with pure determination.

Alfred was drawn to every part of her. He wanted to spoil her rotten. He yearned to sweep her up in his arms and keep her all for himself rather than risk letting her heart be taken by anyone else.

He chided himself for the thought every time. He told himself not to forget that the obsessed king's blood ran through his veins.

Perhaps Iris wouldn't end up like Queen Sharia. After all, she belonged to one of the most influential aristocratic families in Tasmeria. On top of that, she was highly educated. When it came to marriage, she could have her choice of anyone in any country, even another first prince—or Alfred himself.

Rudius had once pointed out that their engagement would benefit both Alfred and House Armelia. But if Alfred loved her, how could he ever ask her to join him on such a dangerous path? If he pursued her before he took care of Ellia, Iris would be targeted with a vengeance.

Even attending the Foundation Day celebration at the queen dowager's express invitation had put Iris in danger. She had restored her reputation, but she was still treated like an outsider.

Moreover, even once the battle for succession was settled, Alfred was afraid of becoming his father. He feared the blood that ran through him, the blood of a man who would clip the wings of the woman he loved to keep her in the cage that was the castle. The man who would tell her: *Look only at me.* Who would tie her down until she suffocated and tear her away from every other person who loved her.

If Alfred did any of that, he would destroy Iris; she would no longer be the free-spirited, independent woman he had fallen in love with. It was a paradox.

At some point, Alfred would have to resume his public role in the royal family. That day wasn't far off now, and it would be the end for them. If Iris couldn't join the royal family by his side, they wouldn't be able to retain their present intimacy. That was why Alfred just wanted to have things go his way, just for a little longer. Iris had taught him how to feel again. He would never leave her, not until he was forced to.

Accomplishments
of the Duke's Daughter

CHAPTER 14

The Duke's Daughter Has a Bad Feeling

"ALL RIGHT, that should do it." I scratched my quill across the paper and signed the last document for the day. "I'm so glad I decided to invite all those truant officials back. There's so much less for me to do now."

I knew it was unseemly, but I slumped over and lay facedown upon my desk. My head was unbearably heavy.

"You did a wonderful job today, my lady." Tanya giggled softly as she set a cup of tea on my desk.

To my surprise, there was a knock at the door, and Dean appeared in the doorway. "Pardon me."

"Dean!" I quickly sat up and hastily patted down my hair. Why did he always insist on dropping in unannounced?

"It's been a long time, my lady."

"Y-yes, it has."

We hadn't seen each other since I met him and Letty. At the time, I'd been annoyed with him—until I realized Letty was his sister. Thinking back on it now, I shouldn't have treated him in such a way. After all, I had no right to tie him down.

When Dean wasn't under contract with me, it wasn't like we were perfect strangers, but we were first and foremost acquaintances. I had no business being angry with him when he was out living his life, even if I had been going through a rough time.

I needed to stop thinking about it, either way. If I thought about it too much, I'd ruminate over my immature reaction to seeing him with Letty, and then I would want to crawl into a hole and die!

"I'm sorry I wasn't able to come when you needed me most," Dean said.

"It's fine. I know you have other responsibilities." I gestured for him to sit down.

Tanya had already prepared some tea for him. Dean took a seat and sipped it while I filled him in on the goings-on in Armelia during his absence. I ended up venting a bit, but he never looked irritated and just listened intently.

"So have you been into town since then?" he asked.

"Hmm? No. I want to go, though." I just hadn't managed to do it, not even after what Mina said. When it came down to actually going through with it, I just kept hesitating. There was also the matter of how much work was on my desk, but...

"You do want to?" Dean asked, and I nodded. "Then I'll do everything I can to help. I know you, and I know if you have even a speck of work left, you'll use that as an excuse not to go."

"Ugh..." He'd said it with a smile, but I had to admit that he'd hit me where it hurt. *Way to call me out, Dean!*

"But since you say you've finished your work, you really should go. It'll just keep bothering you if you don't."

"You're right..." If I kept putting it off, it would get harder and harder to do—*and* it would weigh on me all the while. Then I would drag it out even further. "I'll leave at the next opportunity. Will you help me?"

"Of course." Dean smiled at me.

All right, then. I'd do my best.

"May I have a word?" Dean called out to Tanya in the hallway when she came to take the dishes away.

"What is it?"

Dean casually looked around. When he saw that they were alone, he continued. "You know Dorssen Kataberia, I take it?"

Her gaze grew sharper at hearing the name. "Of course. What about him?"

"I hear he's been lurking around the duchy and Lady Iris. I haven't figured out what he's after yet, though."

"Where did you hear that?"

"From a little bird in the capital. One I met through General Gazell."

"I see." Tanya nodded. If the source was related to the general, then it was a credible one indeed. After all, he was respected deeply not only by the army but also by the knights. "What would you have me do with this information?"

That was the real question. On the surface, Tanya appeared to be nothing more than a maid. Very few people knew that she served Iris in other capacities.

"I wanted to confirm the tip as soon as possible. I knew you would be my best bet in the name of doing so. Am I wrong?"

"Why me?" Tanya pressed.

Dean chuckled. "I can tell just by watching you serve tea that you've been trained in martial arts."

"That's..."

"General Gazell was my master, too. That's how. Moreover, from what I know about you personally, I know that for Lady Iris, you would use your skills to your utmost ability."

"Isn't that what her bodyguards are for?"

"Oh? And you're not one of them? I don't seem to recall discussing the details of anyone's job description."

Tanya frowned for a split second; Dean had her backed into a corner. To be more precise, she had dug herself into a hole.

Dean sensed what she was thinking, and his smile grew stiff. "I've been too forward. What I meant to say was that your movements made clear to me that you have training. The way you observe your surroundings, the way you carry yourself. So it wouldn't surprise me if you were more than simply a maid and if you in fact also acted as Lady Iris's eyes and ears. At least, that would be my guess."

"You're correct." Tanya wasn't sure if she should be questioning her skills or praising Dean's. "Where exactly did you come from?"

It just wasn't right. A man who had only dabbled in martial arts shouldn't have been able to recognize her skills merely from studying her in her duties. She had spent over a decade under the careful tutelage of General Gazell, sharpening her skills. Perhaps Dean had faced someone like her before? That might have explained his ability to recognize Tanya's way of holding herself.

In any other circumstance, she would have made that guess. That was why she doubted it. Why would the son of a merchant belonging to the merchant guild ever expect to be involved in such a fight?

She asked as much; he laughed. There was a darkness in his eyes.

"No matter, then," Tanya said. She could tell she wouldn't get anything else out of him at this rate. "In any case, I'll go ahead and let Lady Iris know."

Dean seemed surprised. "I thought you would confirm the information first."

"I'll look into it, of course, but it's best if she knows right away. Does that surprise you?"

"Yes. I thought you might not want to worry her with unconfirmed information."

"It's unconfirmed, not unreliable." And to be true, there was a time when Tanya would have withheld information for just that reason. However... "Lady Iris stands on her own two feet and moves ever forward. Since I serve her, I cannot stand in her way without a good reason."

Tanya had changed, too, just as Iris had when she resolved herself to be ready for war. Tanya remembered the goosebumps that had rippled down her arms when Iris addressed her truant officials, and she remembered the conversation she'd had with Dida, alone in the middle of a dark night.

Her job wasn't to wrap Iris in silk; it was to follow her mistress's orders and assist her, and at times to serve as her spy. Tanya wouldn't stand in Iris's way just because she wanted to protect her, and so she couldn't cover Iris's eyes and ears either. To do so would be to overstep her bounds.

"I know you wouldn't do that either," Tanya said.

Dean stared at Tanya for a moment, surprised. Then he smiled. "I'm honored to hear you say as much. Well, please go ahead and confirm the information. I'll be awaiting your news."

"I was planning on it."

With that, Dean turned and left. Tanya continued on in the opposite direction, ready to get back to work.

It was truly amazing how fast I got through work with Dean at my side. It was like I'd cloned myself. We muscled through a mountain of backlog in no time at all.

The work had piled up for two reasons. First, I was running a company at the same time as governing a duchy. Second, I was engaged in tens of different projects in the name of reforming Armelia, and all that was on top of my routine work. And then there was how long I'd been away in the capital dealing with the church. And *then* I'd had to deal with the officials on strike.

In other words: Under normal circumstances, I'd never have ended up with such a tremendous backlog, although granted, it wasn't unusual for one or two piles to gather on my desk in the course of running both Armelia and Azuta. At any rate, I made a real dent in the work thanks to Dean. I couldn't help but be impressed with him every time he turned up.

A certain group of government officials groaned whenever Dean arrived, saying things like "Oh, great, the workhorse is here..." and "I should've taken a vacation," while they lamented not being able to go back in time. The only officials who enjoyed his presence were those who worked at Bursa; Dean always managed to get them fired up, and they had all vowed to beat him one day.

What in the world had Dean done to inspire such heated feelings? I'd asked them once, but all they'd done was smile and say, "Only the best of the best work we've ever produced. We can't help but be competitive."

It was true that he was fast at his job, and the officials grew haggard trying to keep up with him. That was how we finished work early enough one day that I was able to go to town.

Tanya did such a good job with my disguise that I hardly recognized myself. She used special makeup techniques that went beyond the normal scope of prettying my face. I also wore glasses, and I used a product from the Azuta Corporation to change my hair color. The last change was shrugging into a cotton frock, and then I was all done. In fact, I looked so different that even those close to me probably wouldn't have been able to tell who I was.

"Let's go, Dean."

"Very well."

"Be careful," Tanya said. She wasn't coming with us; she had something she needed to investigate.

Meanwhile, both Lyle and Dida were presently away from the estate. Dida had gone to east Armelia and Lyle to the north. My initial plan had been to bring multiple guards with me in their stead, but Tanya had been against it. She pointed out that if I had too many guards, no matter how elaborate my makeup, my true identity would be obvious.

Despite Mina's reassurances, I really didn't want to draw any attention to myself. To be honest, I was still a little nervous about having only one guard.

Dean won the responsibility of escorting me, though honestly, he was the best option. He could hold his own against Lyle and Dida, and he wasn't widely recognized in town. Tanya didn't object either. In fact, it sounded like she'd wanted me to bring him in the first place. Something had changed in her lately, and I really had to wonder about that. A change of heart? But that was only part of it.

At any rate, Dean and I went to town together. It was as lively and bustling as usual. Merchants were lined up on the roads, and people strolled down the streets, perusing their wares.

"Ah..." I was so unused to being in crowds again that I accidentally bumped into someone and stumbled. I'd basically been a hermit lately, after all.

Dean caught my arm. "Are you all right?"

"I'm sorry, yes. Thank you." I looked up, feeling embarrassed. Dean's face was closer than I'd imagined it would be. That only made me feel even shyer. Heat rose in my cheeks, and I looked down.

"There are a lot of people here, huh?"

"Y-yes, but I'm glad," I murmured.

Dean smiled tenderly at me—he realized the meaning behind my words. The volume of people meant the economy was good. Things were so stable that they could afford to have leisure time in town. People were only this carefree about shopping in peace times, after all. I had lived in such times in my previous life, and I'd taken scenes like this for granted. Now I knew just how special they were. That was why seeing the town like this felt like proof that I had been doing a good job—and it made me so, so happy.

"We shouldn't just stand here or we'll be in the way," Dean said. "Let's go."

I'd become distracted by the view, but Dean had a point. I was standing smack-dab in the middle of the street.

"You're right, we should go." I made to start walking, but Dean suddenly held his hand out to me. I stared at it in surprise.

"There are so many people here. I don't want you to get lost," he said with a smile.

Right again. I wanted to take his hand, but I was oddly nervous. The hesitation overcame me, and it definitely got a bit weird. Finally, I mustered the courage to take his hand.

Dean's hand was larger than mine, and rougher...and warm. A smile crossed my face. It felt like his warmth traveled straight to my heart. It made me glad. I found myself wishing the moment could last longer—forever.

"Lady Alice, you have some free time today, right?" Dean asked.

"Yes, thanks to you."

"Then let's take a detour," he said, tugging on my hand.

I was a bit surprised, but my foremost feeling was still delight. The grin on my face felt so natural.

"I haven't been here very much." I said as we walked along a street lined with large shops.

"When you used to come, you mostly stuck to the downtown neighborhood or the vicinity of the church."

"I think you're right. But where are we going?"

"I thought it would be good to look at some other shops for a change. The place I most want to take you is a café everyone's been talking about."

"Everyone...from Bursa, you mean?"

"No. I heard about it from Lyle."

"Oh, good. I can't wait."

Dean was still holding my hand as we walked down the street.

I noticed a shop I was interested in. "Let's go in there," I suggested.

"Ah, okay." He seemed oddly reluctant for a moment, so I pulled him along.

It was a jewelry store.

"Welcome," said the employee at the register. Then he spied Dean. "Oh, it's you!"

"Do you know each other?" I glanced at Dean curiously.

"Yes, back when I used to work for the merchant guild. There's something I want to ask him, actually. Is that all right with you?"

"Yes, of course. Go ahead."

He paused before he left. "My lady, please stay inside the shop at all times. This won't take long."

"All right."

Dean disappeared into the back room with the employee. We were still in the same building, and since the jewelry shop had its own guards, I was sure it was fine. I went ahead and browsed the wares.

"Oh, what's this?" I spotted a beautiful pocket watch among the other offerings. It seemed an odd choice for a jewelry store, but as I examined it, I realized gemstones were embedded in the case. "Goodness..."

"Your friend went in the back with the man who runs our sister clock shop," said another employee. "Those watches are the product of our collaboration. I can vouch for the craftsmanship."

I picked up watch after watch to admire them. Each one was better than the last. I was positively entranced.

"These are lovely."

"Thank you. The leaf motif is embossed and set with sapphires. The same color as your eyes, in fact."

"I'll take it, thank you."

"No, thank *you*. Before I wrap it up, I'll get the instructions on its care from the artisan. Could you wait a moment?" I agreed, and the employee went into the back room as well. They said it would take a while, so I chatted with another employee while I looked at the other wares.

"My, are you sure that's the correct price?" I asked with surprise when I heard the total.

"Yes. This shop doesn't cater to the nobility. Our main clientele are from merchant families, such as yourself. We primarily use sapphires, but since no one would buy them loose, we set them in jewelry like so. That drops the price quite a bit."

"Merchant families?"

"Am I wrong? I apologize, I was only guessing because of your friend."

"Oh, that's all right. You were just spot-on, so I was startled. I see. Thank you."

I took the package just as Dean came back into the room, though I quickly hid the package in my purse.

"I'm sorry it took so long," he said.

"That's quite all right. I made the most of my time here."

After that, we kept walking down the street until we ended up at the café we'd originally been aiming for. They had a ton of frozen treats that were the talk of the town. We enjoyed trying various things until we were full.

We had taken our time, and I realized we'd been gone for quite a while. Time really did fly when you were having fun.

As we were walking, something caught my eye, and I stopped.

"What is it?" Dean asked with concern.

I gave him a reassuring smile. "This alleyway just reminds me of someplace."

"Where?"

"Right after I became the acting governor, I took a few companions to tour the domain."

"Dida told me about that."

"That's the one. So anyway, we were in the eastern region of Armelia and I came across a dark alleyway. I started to walk toward it—I was just curious."

"And they stopped you."

"Yes. Dida, specifically. He said I wasn't ready for it yet."

I finally understood what he had meant. It didn't matter how nice and peaceful a place looked on the surface; all it took was one step in the wrong direction, and you might enter a completely different world. A dark world. One where darkness came not from poverty or misfortune, and one that *felt* completely different from how it first appeared.

I'd seen such a place in my past life, too. I'd been walking around idly, feeling excited because I was on a trip. I'd thought being a tourist meant nothing bad could possibly happen to me. I'd been in the middle of a seemingly idyllic town, but when I took a single step into a certain alleyway, the atmosphere had abruptly changed. The people on the streets had turned to me with sharply glinting eyes. The buildings had looked identical to the buildings everywhere else, but I'd been overwhelmed by a heavy, intimidating aura. I had known, instinctually, that I'd walked into a dangerous place.

I remembered being incredibly frightened. To think I'd repeated the same behavior even in my next life! It just went to show how little progress I'd actually made.

At any rate, every town had places where darkness gathered—places where certain organizations were in control. I wouldn't have said such organizations were necessary evils, but they did help maintain order in some neighborhoods. I was glad I hadn't stuck my nose into their business without thinking. Unlike in my past life, I had an important social role in this one, and it was my responsibility to honor that.

Honestly, it was possible that the organizations in Armelia wouldn't entertain the thought of an audience with me even now. They might even eat me alive at the first opportunity. If I really wanted to meet them head-on, I would have to build a system strong enough to surpass them, and I'd have to be powerful enough to force them to abide by it.

"I wonder what Dida would tell me now? That's all I was wondering," I said.

"I'm not sure. Even if you were ready to meet them, Dida would probably give you the same answer. He ran with them once, so he probably wants you to stay far away from that life."

"Wait, you know about that?"

"Yes. I heard a bit about it when I was training with General Gazell."

"I see. And what did you think when you heard?"

"Nothing in particular. It's not that unusual."

"Now I'm curious to know what you *would* consider unusual."

Dean laughed. "Well, I know that Dida has a very keen sense for danger, which he likely learned when he was very little. What about you? What did you think?"

"Nothing, really. No matter who he once was or what he's done, he's never been anything but good to me. And I think who he is now is more important than who he was then. Besides, he's very important to me. He's family."

"I think that's quite wise of you."

"Do you? Ah, look at the time. We should go."

"All right."

We started off again. Our next stop was to visit an old man who owned a restaurant. I was nervous going in, but he didn't recognize me at first. I was once more impressed with Tanya's makeup skills.

When I introduced myself properly, he stared at me blankly. Then he burst into an enormous smile, delighted that I was visiting. In fact, he was so happy that he ordered a free round of drinks for all the customers, on the house—much to his wife's dismay. To be fair, she also greeted me tearfully, and she insisted we would eat for free.

We were greeted warmly everywhere we went, at the florist, at the fishmonger's. One by one, we went to everyone who knew "Alice." None of them said the least word against me. In fact, it was all tearful words of gratitude and heartfelt apologies. Soon, it was so much that I wanted to cry.

"They all adore you," Dean said with a smile on the way home.

From the bottom of my heart, all I could feel was gratitude.

In my past life, I'd devoted all my time to my job. But what had I ever gotten from it? I'd always felt short on time, racing to finish projects at work. My personal relationships had suffered because of it. Money builds up when you don't have time to use it. At some point, you become numb to it all and start to feel like you're in a game.

There was a freedom in the loneliness. It can be easy to live in a world when you're by yourself all the time. It also feels empty.

I still threw myself into my work in Armelia; the difference was that I was so *happy*. Seeing people smile and hearing their kind words meant the world to me. I didn't think it was just because I had a different status. No, I had changed.

I suspected it also had to do with how well my two selves were fusing together. Specifically, the biggest factor was most likely the fact that I had so many experiences to compare and contrast. I'd thrown myself into my next life headfirst, and I wanted to thank God for giving me the chance to be reincarnated.

I looked up at Dean. He noticed my gaze and smiled. I naturally smiled back at him.

"Thank you for today," I said.

"Not at all. I should thank you."

"There's somewhere I'd like to stop before we go home. Is that all right?"

Dean nodded, and it was my turn to take his hand and start walking.

There was a lake on the grounds of the estate, a large one by the forest, that was fed by a small spring inside the woods. The two of us stood at the edge of the spring. The sun had already gone down, and the moon and stars glowed overhead.

"It's beautiful... It's funny how I live here, but for so long, I didn't know I had a view like this," I murmured.

"It is a bit far from the house."

"You're right. I found it once on a walk I took during the afternoon, but it turns out that it's especially beautiful at night."

The full moon and starry sky were reflected in the surface of the water. We were surrounded by trees and quiet, enfolded by serenity.

"Hey, Dean? Thanks. For everything you've done."

"There's no need to thank me, my lady."

"I do need to, though. You connected me with Father Rafsimons, which enabled me to prove my innocence. That's why I want to thank you."

"I did it because I belong to you. But I will gratefully accept your words of gratitude."

"I have more than words to give you. Here, take this." I took out the sapphire-flecked watch I had bought earlier. I'd had them wrap it, so Dean didn't know what was inside.

"My lady...I couldn't possibly accept this," he said with a lop-sided smile.

I pushed it into his hand anyway. "Please. You really did help me so much. And not just with your actions. You helped my heart as well."

"Your heart?"

171

"Yes. I think I was always afraid to show any weakness or let anyone into my heart. I thought it would just cause trouble for them."

Honestly, I was still afraid. I didn't want to get hurt, so I hid my weak self deep inside me—I hid so no one would expect anything from me, and so I wouldn't get my hopes up about anyone either. But being alone was miserably difficult, so I pushed my strong, reliable self to the front.

"I couldn't take it anymore. I hit my limit the day you spoke to me. When you brought out my weaknesses, I was relieved. When you told me it was okay to lean on you, I was so happy, and my heart felt so light. You really saved me. And this is to thank you for that."

"May I open it?"

"Of course."

Dean unwrapped the small package, and his eyes widened with surprise.

"I found it today," I said. "I thought you could use it for work."

"I don't know what to say," he said with a sheepish grin.

The reaction pushed me to the verge of panic—oh, no—

"My lady...I actually have a present for you as well." A determined look came over Dean's face as he handed me a box.

"What?!" I couldn't believe my eyes when I saw it. The box was from the same shop.

"Please open it."

I hesitantly took the box and cracked it open. "Oh, my!"

It was also a watch, but this one was embossed with an exquisite rose, and the gemstones decorating it were a beautiful emerald green—the same color as Dean's eyes.

"It's a congratulatory gift," he said, "as well as an apology."

"An apology?"

"Yes. You thanked me for it, but I was very harsh with you that day. I wanted to apologize. As for congratulations, that's because your conflict with the Church was resolved and you were found innocent."

"But..."

"Please accept it. The owner of that shop is a friend of mine. I wondered why he told me it was on the house, but then... Well, just look."

I did as he said and saw that when you held both pocket watches next to each other, an embossed line seemed to connect the two designs. Mine was a rose, and his was a leaf. The line connecting the two looked like ivy, joining them together.

"Those brothers sure are something," Dean said with a laugh. "They put a lot of thought into this design. I know it may be forward of me, but I dearly want you to keep the other half of it."

My heart was pounding so hard that I was worried I wouldn't be able to survive it. But I smiled, and I accepted the watch. "Thank you. I'm so truly happy..."

"One day, you're going to protect the royal family."

Where had he gone wrong? Whenever Dorssen Kataberia asked himself that, he remembered the words his father had told him every day of his life as he grew up. His father was Doruna

Kataberia, the knight commander of Tasmeria, and he had been training Dorssen ever since he was young.

Dorssen had taken pride in those words, so he had enthusiastically devoted himself to his training. At the same time, growing up like that, he'd thought that entering the academy was incredibly tiresome. He would've rather stayed at home and become a knight's squire instead. Unfortunately, as House Kataberia's only son, he was obligated to attend the academy.

Even after he joined, thanks to his quiet nature, he'd never truly grown used to it. Then one day, he met a girl. Her name was Yuri Neuer. They met on the school training grounds, which the students were free to use as they pleased. Dorssen trained there by himself almost every day.

"That's amazing." This was the first thing she ever said to him.

"What is?"

"Ah, I'm sorry. I come this way every day, over by the edge of the field. So do you, right? I've been wondering what you're doing."

"By the edge?" There was a flower bed in the back of the training grounds, but no path went by it, so it was ill maintained and mostly just weeds.

"Yes. I thought it was a shame that there was such a large flower bed with no flowers, so I've been trying to garden. I got the school's permission, of course."

"You don't have to worry. It's not like I would've reported you or something."

"Well, that's part of it, but...it's a bit unusual for the daughter of a baron to be getting her hands dirty, you know? So I don't really want to talk about it much."

"It's not like you're hurting anyone. I won't say anything either way."

"Thanks. So? What are you doing here every day?" Yuri's smile reminded him of a flower in bloom. For some reason, that warmed him.

"Isn't it obvious?" he asked.

"Well, I can tell that you're training. But I wonder what for? You're already the top student in the martial arts class."

He was taking that course as an elective, as were the other children of knights. Some of them just wanted to learn how to protect their families, while others were second or third sons who dreamed of becoming a knight themselves.

"I'm not training for class."

"You're not?"

"No. I'm training so that I can offer my services to the royal family."

Yuri stared at him blankly for a few moments, then she smiled deeply. "That's wonderful. I bet it would feel so wonderfully reassuring to be protected by someone like you."

Those words and that smile left a lasting impression on Dorssen.

From time to time, Yuri would come to visit him while he was training. They would chat a bit, and then she would leave. At first, he didn't think anything of it, but gradually, he found himself looking forward to seeing her. She would compliment things that came naturally to him, telling him that he was wonderful. That he was amazing.

He found those compliments so encouraging that they made him even more enthusiastic about his exercise. He thought multiple times that he would love to devote his sword to her. Every time he chided himself, reminding himself that his sword was meant for the royal family.

By the time Dorssen realized he was in love with Yuri, she was already engaged to Prince Edward. At first he was depressed, but his desire to protect her won out. He realized that he could love her even while missing her, and that somewhat healed his heart.

Even better, he realized he would now be able to dedicate himself to her protection. During the conflict between Iris, Yuri, and Edward, he had of course taken Yuri's side. Iris's expulsion had been in the name of protecting Yuri. So he'd thought, at least.

"What have you done?" Doruna, his father, asked in an incredibly stern tone.

Dorssen didn't know what he meant and gave him a puzzled look.

His father heaved a sigh. "I'm talking about the duke's daughter!"

"Why are you yelling?"

"Are you serious?"

"Yes."

"I can't believe you'd raised a hand to the duke's daughter—even worse, you aspire to become a knight, and you raised your hand to a woman, period! Where is your pride in our chivalric code?"

"But the duke's daughter was abusing Lady Yuri."

"And did you see her doing it?"

"W-well, not directly, but everyone said—"

"And did you investigate these claims to ensure their verity? Did you witness any of it with your own eyes?"

"N-no..."

"I'm so furious, I don't even know what to say! You raised a hand to a woman without proof! To the fiancée of the second prince! You don't *deserve* to be a knight! You've brought shame both on this house and on the knighthood itself!"

"But I—"

"I'll hear none of your excuses! I order you to stay at home until you've cooled off that damn head of yours!"

With that, Doruna ordered the butler to escort Dorssen to his room and confine him there. For a good long while, Dorssen was not allowed to attend school, which meant he was unable to train. He had nothing to do besides sit in his room and think.

Dorssen had no idea why he was being punished. All he'd wanted was to protect Yuri. After he had been confined for a set period of time, his father allowed him to resume his training but forbade him from seeing Yuri. This just led Dorssen to distrust his father's judgment even more.

It wasn't until after he saw Yuri again at the Foundation Day celebration that he came to understand his father's sentiment.

His mother summoned him to meet with her after the party. "It's good to see you again, Dorssen."

"Hello, Mother," he said as the butler placed a teacup and a plate in front of him.

"That's called chocolate. It's quite popular in the capital now. Try it," his mother urged.

Dorssen had never seen anything like this food before, and he took a bite.

"It was made by the company House Armelia owns."

"House Armelia..."

"Just as the queen dowager said, the one running the company is Lady Iris. The daughter of Duke Armelia." Lady Kataberia seemed sad when she said Iris's name. "Dorssen, can you really hold your head high and say you did the right thing?"

"What do you mean?"

"Honestly, your actions have led to some significant political difficulties for our house. But putting that aside, do you really think you did the *right thing*?"

Her question puzzled him. Dorssen didn't know what she *meant*. He thought he'd done the right thing, without a doubt. But he had been punished, and his father had told him he had brought shame to the entire knighthood.

Did this mean his father had been angry merely because Dorssen had caused social problems for House Kataberia? If so, then he was even more convinced than ever of the rightness of his actions. As long as he protected Yuri, he didn't care what happened to his family.

"Really, Dorssen, and this might sound rude, but...I feel sorry for the duke's daughter."

"And why is that, Mother?"

"Because Yuri Neuer set her eyes on a man who was already engaged and stole him away from Lady Iris. As a woman, I can understand why Lady Iris reacted like she did. Another woman grew close to her fiancé for malicious reasons. She felt jealous and threatened. Who could blame her for speaking against Yuri?"

"Well..."

"Yuri stole away the person she loved. And for it, you humiliated her in front of the entire academy, and now she's been exiled from high society."

Dorssen thought back to the final confrontation they'd had with Iris.

Ms. Yuri. What more do you wish to steal from me? You've taken my fiancé, my position... She'd said this while tears welled in her eyes.

"It seems to me that these chocolates are a symbol of her determination," said his mother. "Her determination to make it alone, without marrying. Her engagement was broken, and she was written off by the aristocracy. It will indeed be difficult for her to find another respectable union. And Dorssen...you raised a hand to her, participated in her humiliation, and supported the woman who instigated her fall to ruin. So, as a knight, can you really say you did the right thing?"

"Well..." Dorssen couldn't argue with that. He hadn't thought about it. It was so obvious, yet he'd never considered Iris's pain—or her sadness, which must have been insurmountable.

"Are you satisfied that you protected the woman you love? Is that what you honed your skills for?" His mother shook her head. "Dorssen, I really wouldn't believe something until I saw proof of it myself. And what I saw at the celebration was you speaking to Prince Edward and Yuri—and that you confronted Lady Iris. What was that all about? Were you really speaking ill of Lady Iris just to gain someone else's attention? Is that how a knight treats a lady?"

Every word Dorssen's mother spoke twisted the knife lodged in his heart. There was no going back now.

"I'm no knight," she went on, "so perhaps I don't understand the code or your vows. But at the celebration, I saw you treat Lady Iris with what I could only call outright abuse."

When Dorssen's father had scolded him, he'd only felt rebellious. Now his heart was filled with confusion and regret.

"I hope you feel ashamed of yourself."

Following his meeting with his mother, Dorssen devoted every hour of his days to training. He needed to clear his head. All he could think of were his mother's words—and Iris's. He was in torment.

As a result, he became alienated from Prince Edward and Yuri. After graduation, he joined the knights as a squire, just as he had planned. He sparred with the other knights, and every day was more fulfilling than the last. He'd always longed to join their order. The knighthood was everything to him, and since his values had wavered, he was even more attached to the idea of becoming one.

Soon enough, the knighthood became his entire world.

During that time, General Gazell's two apprentices started coming to participate in joint drills between the knights and the army. The apprentices of General Gazell—the living hero. Dorssen had been jealous of them, though no more so than everyone else around him. The general's chosen apprentices were the envy of every soldier and knight alike.

However, Dorssen had trained for the knighthood ever since his boyhood, so he was more than confident in his skills. Moreover, he was unbelievably proud to have at last joined the order. Yet he just couldn't find it in himself to blithely accept the general's apprentices. So he challenged them.

"I don't know how much pride you take in being a knight. But I don't consider you one."

With those words, Dida had handed Dorssen an overwhelming defeat.

Dorssen was frustrated, and he even despaired, much to his chagrin. What had he worked so hard for? Dida's words had been the terrible echo of his mother's. He began to fear that he had wasted his time aspiring to be a knight.

"Huh? You wanna know about Lyle and Dida?" one of his superiors asked, though he looked surprised. "Why don't you ask 'em yourself? Just say, 'Please tell me more about yourselves!'"

"No, I don't think so..."

"Well, I can't blame you, after that fight. You left the worst first impression," the knight chuckled. "Well? What do you wanna know about them?"

"I want to know why they haven't come to the capital to enlist. They would be welcomed into the ranks of the knights or the soldiers. So why haven't they?"

"Don't you remember what they said? They've devoted their swords to the mistress who saved them. Their loyalty to her is greater than their own pride. Seems to me they're truer knights than we are. Oh—right, their mistress is Duke Armelia's daughter, Lady Iris."

"What? *She's* their mistress?" Dorssen asked.

The knight frowned. "You don't seem happy to hear that."

"No, it's just that…I kept wondering who it was they served. I never would have guessed it was Lady Iris."

"You went to school with her, didn't you?"

"Yes. …What do you think of her?"

"Don't ask me. I've never spoken with her beyond a hello. You know her better."

"The things people say about her…are unflattering."

"I know that much. You must be talking about the incident that led to her expulsion. My family's of the nobility, too, you know."

"So you know, then."

"That's it, though, right?"

"Well…" Dorssen paused. Wasn't her expulsion proof enough?

"People are more complicated than they seem. They show different sides of themselves, depending on the time and place."

"Isn't that a bit deceptive?"

"Is it? Let me ask you this—are you the same at home as you are when you're here with us?"

"Well..."

"I know I'm not. That's why I can't say what kind of person she is. Haven't been around her enough. I'm not saying I'd just ignore the things I've heard about her. But on one hand, you've got the evil villainess who harassed the daughter of a baron, and on the other, you've got the benevolent mistress who saved Lyle and Dida, to whom they feel so indebted that they've devoted their lives to her. Which one's the truth? What kind of person do *you* think she is?"

Honestly, Dorssen couldn't answer. He'd never been around Iris long enough to share stories about her. Everything he knew about her was something he'd heard from someone else. He had based his entire opinion on hearsay. "I..."

That was as far as he got. The knight frowned at him and shrugged.

Dorssen kept thinking about it. He thought of his father's words, and his mother's, and the knight's. No matter how much he thought, he kept coming to the same conclusion: that as a *man*, he had done nothing wrong. He still couldn't forgive Iris for what she had done, and he had no intentions of doing so. At the same time, he had come to think he might have done the wrong thing as a *knight*.

It was incontrovertibly true that he had humiliated Iris and disrespected her in public. He believed he should apologize to her for that. He tried to meet with her to do so, but no matter how many times he requested a meeting, he was turned away. He even began to approach the Armelia mansion in the capital, but they never let him past the gate.

He asked his friend for advice again, to which the man responded, "Are you stupid or something?"

They were at the tavern in town. It wasn't really the kind of place two nobles would go, but due to General Gazell's influence, they'd taken to visiting the establishment for a drink after work.

"Let me ask you this: What if Lady Iris said, 'I don't feel bad about what I did, but I apologize for responding inappropriately as the daughter of a duke.' What would you do?"

"Well...I don't know. I just want to settle things."

"Settle things? Obviously, she's gonna be suspicious if you start coming around suddenly, saying you want to see her. Hell, is your apology even sincere? Anyway, if you think she's got the time to listen to you, you're crazy."

"I do mean it, though. I feel terrible about my behavior. It was unbecoming of a knight."

"That's it, though. Remember what I asked you? About how you'd feel if the situation were reversed? How *would* you feel?"

Dorssen wasn't sure how to answer, though he wanted to. When he thought of Yuri's suffering, he just couldn't forgive Iris for what she'd done. He would think any apology empty and meaningless.

His expression said it all to his friend, who nodded. "See? You wouldn't really mean your apology. Your heart's not in it. If you try to apologize and it's not real, they're gonna know it." Then the knight's face grew serious. "Anyway, apologizing might feel good because then you feel like it's all over, but it doesn't feel that way for the person you wronged. They have to decide whether they're going to forgive you, and if you get another chance. So are you going to be selfish? You going to let your own feelings cause her even more pain?"

It wouldn't be easy to settle this, not at all. At least, that was what Dorssen felt his friend was trying to say. The other knight seemed to think that Dorssen's desire to apologize was presumptuous in itself.

"Then what should I do?" Dorssen asked.

"Don't look at me. What do you *want* to do? I keep asking you that. Because from here, it seems like you just want to make yourself feel better by offering her empty words—and not even because you feel bad, but because you're getting swept up in what everyone else says. You need to think about it yourself. Think deeper and with a more open mind. What do you want to do? What *can* you do?"

They drank for a little longer after that and then went their separate ways.

Once Dorssen got home, he kept replaying the conversation with his friend in his mind.

He thought about everything that had happened and everything that might happen. He thought about it over and over again, about what he'd done and about what he wanted to do. He thought and thought, but he couldn't come to a conclusion, until finally...

"I want to learn more about her."

That was Dorssen's resolution. He didn't know anything about Iris, which meant he needed to learn. He wanted to know what she had really done and what she really wanted to do. So he took leave from the knights and embarked on a journey to learn the truth of this Iris Lana Armelia.

CHAPTER 15

The Duke's Daughter
Makes Her Move

"**M**Y LADY, Dorssen has entered Armelia," Tanya told me one night with a sigh.

I'd been puzzled when Dean told me about Dorssen, but thanks to his warning, I was able to take the news calmly. "Keep an eye on him. If he acts in a remotely suspicious way, stop him immediately."

"Yes, my lady."

"Why is he coming here *now*?" To be honest, all I wanted to do was arrest and deport him. "What about his work?"

"He took leave from the order."

"So he's just doing as he pleases? Honestly, what is Doruna thinking?"

"Perhaps he thought it wasn't a good idea for him to remain with the knights? The knights are everything to Doruna, and he has utmost pride in and respect for them. Despite that pride, he seems to understand that Dorssen went too far. But Dorssen is his only son, so...perhaps he's giving him one last chance before disinheriting him."

"That's awfully generous..." I had to laugh. "Well, no matter. I won't let him do as he pleases, that's for sure." I squeezed my hand into a fist.

"How was your trip to town, by the way?"

"What? What do you mean?!" The sudden change in subject flustered me.

"You've just been in such a good mood since you came back, is all."

"Oh! Um, yes..." Tanya was wildly perceptive, and the accuracy of her insight took me off guard. I definitely overreacted. Ack. "I...am very happy. I feel most fortunate." That was all I could think to say.

"I see." Tanya smiled.

"More importantly..." I said abruptly. The topic of going into town had reminded me of something. "Let's say you made a terrible mistake. Something truly bad that you couldn't take back. What if you found yourself about to be in the same position as when you had made that mistake the first time?"

"That's a difficult question," Tanya said with a frown. "Does finding myself in the same position mean I'm guaranteed to make the same mistake?"

"I don't know. But—just imagine that it was the worst mistake ever."

"I suppose I can't say I'd have to try and see." Tanya closed her eyes. She was taking this seriously. After a moment of silence, she said, "I suppose I would think of the things I would stand to gain and the things I might lose. If the matter wasn't too important, then I'd try to find a way to avoid it wholesale. If I was reluctant to do so, that would mean there was something about this position—something beyond the mistake—that was hard for me to let go of. A hope I couldn't abandon. So I would try to have it both ways. A mistake means I took a risk—that I might have gained something, even if I lost it the first time. If I avoid the decision entirely, then I guarantee that I lose that thing—and I might even lose something I already have."

"Hope you can't abandon..."

"Yes. This is only a hypothetical, but I believe I understand what you're trying to say. If you found yourself in a similar position, I would support you in whatever decision you made. We would continue to push our way forward, and everyone else would do the same. We all have our own way of doing things, and even if we don't entirely agree with a choice you make, we still support *you*. And if you find yourself trapped, not knowing what to do, please think of us—and use us. Does that answer satisfy you, my lady?"

"Yes, more than enough. Thank you. ...But I'm exhausted, so I think I'll retire for the night."

"All right."

Tanya helped me get ready for sleep. Once she left, I got out of bed and walked to the balcony. It was unbecoming of me, as I wore only my thin nightgown, but no one would see me in the dark.

I looked up at the night sky and then toward the town. The dark worked against me as well; I couldn't see much. With electricity yet undiscovered in this world, the nights were very dark. At the same time, I found it comforting.

"Hope you can't abandon... Ridiculous." I gritted my teeth.

I couldn't hold back the tears anymore, but thankfully, I didn't need to worry that anyone would see me cry out here. My whispers faded into the darkness. I just kept crying, more and more. Even though I was clenching my teeth, stifled sobs leaked out.

I wasn't mocking Tanya's words. In fact, I felt not the least bit of spite for them. She had skewered me.

There was indeed a hope buried deep in my heart that I couldn't abandon. *I* was ridiculous.

I'd endured so much pain, so I'd locked those feelings away. Yet here, they'd surfaced again so easily. I was so *fragile*. Now I knew that, even though I'd tried to deny it. I gave myself every excuse and lied to myself at every opportunity. But the truth was obvious.

Why did I rely on him so much? Why had I let him see so much of me? Why did I allow him to see my pain, even when I hid my emotions from others? Why had I felt such jealousy?

My heart knew the answer to all those questions, but I had refused to let my brain accept it.

I clutched the pocket watch he'd given me. It was nothing but a hazy outline in the darkness. Only the cold of it in my hands let me know that it was in fact there.

I couldn't make the same mistake. I couldn't afford to lose.

I couldn't lose the people who followed me, or Armelia, or the citizens who lived there. They were all too precious to risk—and I was too frightened to remember the despair I'd experienced when I'd last been betrayed, and too afraid of being foolish enough to expose myself again.

I didn't want that. I didn't want *this*.

Why did that dreadful uncertainty, invisible and intangible, against which I had been so powerless, have to come over me again? Why were these feelings so intense, so overwhelming? I was terrified.

"I love you." My heart dropped when I said the words aloud. Words I could never say in front of him—because nothing could ever come of them.

Love that surpassed social status was a fairy tale. Although, even Cinderella was an aristocrat. And Yuri was the daughter of a baron.

So I couldn't tell him.

I couldn't abandon the things that were precious to me. Therefore, I had to lie to my heart. I had to turn my back on all this. Come morning, I would wake up and I'd return to the world with a smile on my face.

"The numbers don't add up. If you compare them to the last report, exports *and* imports...have decreased." I bit my lip in concern as I pointed out the discrepancies. "I wonder why? It's not everyday goods; it's the luxury imports. And they've only decreased in the eastern region of Armelia."

"You're very perceptive," the Bursa official said, eyes widening.

"I hate to admit it, but I didn't notice until Dean pointed it out, actually," I said with a chuckle. "What did you think? Did you assume I wouldn't catch it?"

"Is this a test?"

"I don't know. I'm just curious. I like to know what my employees think of me. Speaking of Dean, I thought he was writing a report on this. Do you know what's going on with that?"

"It hasn't come in yet. Dean is investigating the cause of the discrepancy and sent someone east to check on things. As to your question—I was sure you would see it. Dean said so too, when he handed me the documents."

"Ah! So *Dean* was testing me!" I laughed.

"Are you angry?"

"No, it's amusing. But I really do wonder why this is happening. It isn't like the population has dropped off. And demand hasn't gone down either. The prices are still high across the board. This isn't happening anywhere else but in that region. Could it be that someone's manipulating the supply chain?" I mused as I flipped through the documents.

The Bursa official watched me as I did, waiting for his next instructions. I thanked him for the report, and he took his leave.

"Call Sebastian," I said to Tanya.

As soon as Sebastian arrived, I gave him my orders. I wanted everything he had on the situation in the east. That was where Armelia's main port lay, so it was a wealthy and busy region. It had only grown more so since I'd become acting governor, especially as we were putting more effort into developing relationships with other countries.

Revenue from the east was integral to Armelia's ongoing financial health; I had to get to the bottom of this. I wouldn't feel at ease until I did. At present, the situation was only affecting one type of good, but there was no guarantee that the problem wouldn't spiral into other areas.

"Dean, I just received the reports. How are things progressing?" I asked when he arrived as well.

"Honestly, there's nothing new to say. I sent people to investigate the situation, and I'm waiting for news. One thing has been bothering me, however."

"Is it that there doesn't seem to be anything out of the ordinary besides the numerical discrepancy?"

"Yes. It's too quiet out there. No reports of a ship sinking, no rogue companies. No complaints from the businesses producing the goods. Even though someone, somewhere should be suffering because of the dip in profits, we've heard nothing. It's strange."

"If only we could dismiss this. But I have a bad feeling about it. How long did you say you could stay this time?"

"My original contract expires tomorrow. I have an appointment I must keep, so I'll be away from Armelia for about a week, but I can come back as soon as I'm done. Sebastian can take over in my absence, along with the official from Bursa who was just here—the fellow who brought the reports."

"All right... I suppose it can't be helped." If I were being honest,

I would've felt much better if Dean could have stuck around. But it wasn't good to rely on him so much. "All right. If you think of anything new or something changes, let me know."

I headed to the library next. I was grateful we had discovered this issue while Dean was still here. I'd had so much work piled up before his arrival that I wouldn't have been able to respond to it promptly. I might not even have noticed it without him. Thanks to him, I'd finished the backlog, but he'd spotted this issue in the first place—then run it by the official who'd come to me with the report. Either way, I was grateful to him.

I arrived at the library and entered. "Oh, Rehme! It's been a while since I saw you here."

"Lady Iris!" Rehme greeted me with a bright smile. She was my librarian, but the academy in Armelia was keeping her busy with requests, so lately, she hadn't spent as much time at the estate as usual. To be fair, I barely had time to go to our library myself, so it really had been a long time since I'd seen her in her usual habitat, surrounded by books.

"What brings you here, my lady?"

"Just doing some research about eastern Armelia."

"What exactly are you looking for? Cuisine? Oh, how about maps?"

"I'm looking for historical records, like a list of the mayors of the port town. Criminal records too, that sort of thing."

"Here's information on the mayors. It hasn't been bound into a book, so it's quite fragile. Please be careful with it."

"All right, thank you." I took the packet of papers from Rehme.

"And here are the criminal records. There's not much to them, actually. The vast majority of it gets covered up, I expect."

"Oh? I suppose I heard that before we had a standing police force, crimes weren't recorded except for major incidents, which is understandable. What do you mean by covered up, though?"

"Eastern Armelia has always attracted hotheads, what with its port. Fights and brawls are daily occurrences. Not to mention, the Boltik family controls things, so anything really big gets swept under the rug, and we don't hear about it out here."

"The Boltik family? Who's that?" I'd never heard of them before.

"To put it simply, an organization that controls the underworld. Do you remember when Dida stopped you from walking down that alleyway? The sort of people you would have met there."

"I see. If I had Tanya investigate their recent activities, do you think we'd be able to discern whether anything had changed for them recently?"

"Well, the family dates back a very long time. Probably since the duchy was established and the port was built. They have their own way of doing things, and even though they commit some... indiscretions, the citizens don't seem to dislike them."

"What do you mean by that?"

"Illegal activities. Not slavery, though. They do have people guarding their operations—likely gambling, for the most part."

"I see. If they employ guards, then you're probably right—they resolve conflicts before we ever hear of them. And what sense does it make to record an event if it's settled before anyone uninvolved ever learns it happened?"

"Something like that."

"You sure know a lot, Rehme."

"We've gathered a handful of records on the various heads of the family throughout the years. It's all quite interesting."

"I see. It would be dangerous to investigate someone like that on your own, wouldn't it? Just thinking about it gives me the shivers."

I had a feeling it was going to take a great deal of effort to get to the bottom of this. It would have been different if I'd read anything about it before, but even now that I had the material, it would be no mean feat to get through it all. It made me incredibly grateful to have Rehme at my disposal.

"Are there other organizations like the Boltiks?"

"Of course, several. Although I don't know how many are still around, especially after some went toe to toe against the Boltik family."

"Well, then... Thank you."

Late at night, Dida spotted a certain someone leaving the mansion. "Wait, Tanya."

"What is it, Dida? I'm busy." Tanya glared at him, but his usual carefree smile remained fixed on his face.

"I know. Princess told you to go investigate out east, right?

And you've gotta do that on top of keeping an eye on the spoiled rich boy. Must be rough."

"If you know I'm busy, then let me go."

"Don't have to."

"Huh?"

"I'm coming with. You know what they say, every man knows his own business best. Guess I'm headed to my old stomping grounds."

Dida's words reminded Tanya of his experiences. Iris had adopted him while she was on a trip in the east with her family. At the time, Tanya had been apprenticed as a maid, so she had stayed behind at the estate. She didn't know the particulars of the trip, only that Dida was from the east and that he had belonged to a criminal organization during that time.

"Don't you have your own work to do?" she asked.

"I've got a very talented partner. And anyway, I have apprentices now. Plenty of people to pick up the slack."

"Well, you can't. I'm looking into your old acquaintances, and they might recognize you. It's too dangerous."

"Hey, now. You know I can take care of myself."

"I'm aware. You don't have to remind me. But why? Why do you want to come?"

"Because I'll do anything to help Princess. And like I said, I know the lay of the land."

Tanya stared at Dida, trying to discern his motives. He just stared back at her, smiling. But the look in his eyes was deadly serious.

"Let's say I've got a bad feeling about this," he said. "That's why I want to go myself and see what's really happening. And if I can settle some things at the same time, then good."

"Do you really think I'd let you come after hearing that?"

"Like I said, I can handle it. ...Which is to say, sorry about this."

That was when Tanya felt the impact. She chastised herself for letting her guard down as her consciousness slipped away. The last thing she saw was the culprit's face and the apology in his gaze.

The next time she opened her eyes, she was for a moment confused. She saw the ceiling of her room, just like she always did upon waking. But none of that had been a dream. She was still wearing the clothes she'd had on when she left the house. She rose and rushed to Iris's room to inform her of what had happened.

"Dida took over the investigation?" Iris looked surprised. "I know I shouldn't worry about him, but I'm afraid he'll do something rash... But Lyle's the only person who could bring him back, and we can't spare the number of people we'd need to cover for him. Honestly...I'm grateful Dida's chosen this. Why don't we just wait and see what happens?"

Tanya couldn't bring herself to speak out against Iris's judgment. "Very well, my lady."

She suppressed the unpleasant feeling smoldering within her and returned to her work.

Dorssen had arrived in Armelia. He was genuinely surprised to see that its capital was as fine and boisterous as the royal capital itself. In fact, he'd been nothing but surprised since he entered the duchy. A long line of people had been waiting to gain entrance into Armelia. Once Dorssen passed through the gates, he had been continually impressed by the well-maintained roads and other orderly affairs.

In other domains, city roads were well maintained, but farther afield, the roads were often neglected. In Armelia, every road between every settlement was exceptionally well taken care of, which made travel across the domain incredibly easy. Furthermore, outposts housing soldiers from Armelia's ducal army were stationed at intermittent points along the roads, and regular patrols ensured the safety of all travelers.

Dorssen found himself thinking, *No wonder so many prime ministers have hailed from Armelia.*

As soon as he reached the duchy's capital, he booked a room at an inn and wandered the town for a while. He grew curious when he noticed a steady stream of people entering a large building.

"Excuse me. What's in that shop there?" he asked a man passing by.

"Shop? Are you a tourist?"

"You could say that..."

"That's a branch of our academy. The elementary school, to be exact. All the children of Armelia learn how to read and write there, free of charge. Mathematics as well."

"That's...that's amazing." It was indeed amazing, but, Dorssen wondered, was it necessary? Reading, writing, and arithmetic only seemed like relevant skills to the children of aristocrats or merchants. What use would an ordinary citizen have for such things?

"It is!" the passerby exclaimed. He seemed delighted by the opportunity to tell an out-of-towner all the exciting things about the school. "It's a new program that started after Lady Iris became the acting governor. She says 'knowledge is power,' and everyone deserves to be able to stand on their own two legs—make a living for themselves, you know? At first, I thought it was crazy, but once you really start learning, it hits you. Knowledge opens up more possibilities for your future. You can get a better job, for instance, and you can use these things in your daily life, too!"

"Lady Iris... The duke's daughter is the acting governor?"

"Indeed she is. After she took office, she built us more hospitals, reformed our tax system, and all sorts of things that have made our lives a damn sight easier."

Dorssen had not known about Iris's responsibilities—not in the least. "Do you go to that academy, too?"

"Sure do. At the moment, I'm studying to enter their branch for higher education."

Dorssen thanked the man and started talking to other passersby as well. No one seemed particularly displeased with the fact that a woman was running the duchy. In fact, they seemed to think it was perfectly natural. Everything they had to say about Iris was positive, and some even gushed about her like the first man he'd spoken to. She seemed to be beloved by her citizens, and it didn't take Dorssen long to be sure this was the case.

In fact, she was so popular that a dark feeling began to congeal within his heart. They spoke of Iris as if she were some kind of saint, but this same woman had abused Yuri. How could they idolize her like this?

Dorssen was speaking to the owner of a restaurant, a man who'd given yet another glowing review of Iris, when he snapped. "Excuse me," he said. "I realize that Lady Iris has done a number of things for Armelia, but why does everyone *love* her so much?"

"That's a strange question. She always acts in our best interests, and she truly cares about us. How could we not love someone like that?"

"Yes, but haven't you heard about how when she lived in the capital, she abused our future queen? They expelled her from the academy for it. How could you believe someone like that cares about you and your livelihood? Are you sure she's really behind all this? Isn't it more likely that it's the people working for her?"

The shop owner burst out laughing. "That whole business? I'm sure it was a misunderstanding. Probably another setup like when the church excommunicated her over a false accusation. No, we feel extremely fortunate to have her as our governor."

"How can you trust her so?"

"Listen, it doesn't matter what you say. I've seen what she can *do*. She works her tail off for Armelia, and she visits the orphanage even though she's so busy—matter of fact, she comes and visits everyone in town. I don't think anyone cares more about us than she does, that's for sure!"

"But..."

"What about you? What do you know about her? I think you'd better watch what you say. The people here adore their Lady Iris. They won't take well to hearing anyone badmouth her. Look around. You've got some glares on you, my friend."

Dorssen looked over his shoulder and realized the man was right; several of the other patrons were staring at him, and not in a friendly way. They glared with something that very closely resembled malice.

"My apologies."

"You just be careful," the owner said before walking away.

Iris truly was loved by her citizens. Had she had a change of heart after her expulsion or something?

Dorssen paid his bill and left the restaurant. Even though the sun had gone down, people were still milling about the town. That indicated that they felt safe doing so. Between this and everything else he'd seen and heard, Dorssen was actually starting to wonder if Iris really had abused Yuri.

He quickly shoved that thought out of his mind. He couldn't doubt Yuri, after all. There was no way she would lie. In fact, it was a good thing that she'd spoken up—the whole incident had no doubt caused this change in Iris's character.

Dorssen returned to his room at the inn and stared absently at the view from his window while he drank some ale. Why had he come here to begin with? To learn more about Iris, yes, but what had he planned on doing with that information once he got it? Honestly, he didn't know what he wanted anymore. Did he still want to settle things?

If so, why did he want that? It had occurred to him that he might have gotten carried away. His father and mother had placed so much blame upon him, so of course he had wanted to fix things between himself and the woman who was now the queen dowager's favorite. But he had only wanted to do so for the sake of appearances. He had wanted to excuse his behavior, to be able to say, "I apologized. I settled it."

"What do you want to do? I keep asking you that. Because from here, it seems to me like you just want to make yourself feel better by offering her empty words—and not even because you feel bad, but because you're getting swept up in what everyone else says. You need to think about it yourself. Think deeper and with a more open mind. What do you want to do? What can you do?"

His friend's advice kept circling through his head.

His friend was right. Dorssen hadn't thought about Iris at all, even though she was the one to whom he owed an apology.

What *was* an apology? What did it mean to 'settle things'? Dorssen let out a deep sigh and looked away from the window. His mug had been empty for a while now. He headed downstairs, ready to order another drink from the bar on the first floor.

Every other inn in town was full, and Dorssen had secured the last room. The bar was overflowing with people.

"You traveling alone?" a man asked just as Dorssen was about to place an order.

"Yeah, that's right."

"Did you come here to shop? Doesn't look like it. Got a girl here?"

"Not quite. What about you?"

"Me? I came for the goods, but unfortunately..."

"Did you run into some kind of trouble?"

"They ran out of what I was looking for. It was an import. Seems there's some kind of trouble in the east."

"What do you mean?"

"Well, some ruffians called the Boltik family are throwing their weight around. It's grown too dangerous to even travel out that way."

"What's the government doing about it?"

"The governor's mobilizing the armed forces. I'm sure they'll resolve it pretty soon."

"Are Armelia's soldiers that powerful?"

"Sure are. Not even the knights in the capital would stand a chance against them!"

"What...?"

"Don't glare at me like that. It's just a hypothetical. You know a knight or something?"

"No, sorry. I just admire them, is all."

"Oh, I see. Sorry about that. Well, why don't you go and see them in action for yourself? If you admire the knights, I bet you'd learn a lot watching the Armelia's soldiers. You look strong enough to protect yourself out east anyway."

"I wonder if Dida's going," Dorssen murmured.

The man didn't hear him and gave him a questioning look.

"Ah, it's nothing," said Dorssen. "Is the east usually better-traveled?"

"Sure is. It's real important for our trade. Rumor has it that it was the first place Lady Iris visited when she became acting governor."

"Interesting."

"It's also the most popular tourist destination in the duchy. If you came here on a vacation, I'd recommend them or the south! Then you'll really be able to see how much progress Lady Iris has made here."

"I see. Thanks for the info." Dorssen returned to his room, thinking. "The east, huh?"

Maybe it would do him some good to continue traveling Armelia. Retrace Iris's footsteps, as it were. He downed his second mug of ale and went straight to bed.

"Have you heard anything from Dida?" I asked. It had been two weeks since he left, but he'd sent no word so far as I knew. With every day that passed, another old worry resurfaced.

"No," said Tanya.

"I see... What about from our other investigation party?"

"They said that conditions in the port town are deteriorating. If we haven't heard anything directly, that means the residents are afraid to speak out against the Boltik family. They could also be colluding with the local officials."

"I see. What exactly does the Boltik family want in this situation? Are they angling for a direct fight with me? I mean, House Armelia?"

"I think that's unlikely. Their current boss has been the head of the family for some time, and it's hard to believe he'd move against us so suddenly."

"That's true. Might it be possible that someone is impersonating the Boltik family...?"

"My lady..." Tanya frowned. "There's something else."

"What is it?"

"I've heard Dorssen has set out on a journey eastward."

"Huh?"

"He left town this morning. I thought he was returning home, but he headed in the other direction, toward the east. I didn't believe it, at first, but..."

"Why would he go there now, of all times? I thought he came to Armelia to talk to me, didn't he?"

"It honestly doesn't make sense. But for now, here's a list of the people he sought out in town."

I took the paper from Tanya and looked it over. No suspicious names jumped out. But...

"Look into this merchant's activities one more time. And put more eyes on Van."

"On Van?"

"Yes, please. I don't trust Dorssen's decision to go east—it can't be coincidence. Perhaps he hopes to negotiate with some individuals out there. It would be too early for him to act, either way.

But we can't assume he's come for a good reason. Go check with Father Rafiel as well—and if you've time, investigate the behavior of our local aristocracy."

Just then, there was a knock at the door.

"Dean." I smiled. "You have impeccable timing."

"Forgive me, my responsibilities ran a bit long and I've returned later than I anticipated."

I filled him in on the situation, and his face grew grave as I described it.

"While I was away, I heard some suspicious rumors," he said. "They say one of your trusted people is in truth a ruffian—that he's trying to extort money from the citizenry. Other rumors say that a former classmate of yours, one who joined the knights, is trying to rectify the situation. That's most of it."

"Where did these rumors start?"

"I'm looking into it now. I thought perhaps some noble was saying things to get a rise out of you, but if that were the case, it would be strange for word to be circulating among the townspeople."

"I see..."

"My lady, Dida..." Tanya had been listening quietly the entire time, but now she spoke up.

I shook my head. "I trust Dida. Or at least...I want to. More than anything, I'm genuinely worried about him. I think we should take care of this before it grows any bigger."

I needed to determine my next steps. I told Tanya to summon Sebastian.

"May I help you, my lady?" he asked when he arrived.

"Sebastian, I'm going to be away for about a week. I'll leave my business in your care until I return."

"Yes, my lady. I will do my utmost to fulfill my duties." Sebastian frowned a bit at my order, but he nevertheless bowed his head.

"My lady, are you…"

"Indeed I am. I'm going east. Luckily, I don't have much of a backlog, so Sebastian can take the reins for now." I smiled. "Honestly, I've overworked myself to the point of exhaustion. I must recuperate. Sebastian will look after things in my stead. Do you understand what I mean?"

"Yes," said Tanya. "And you won't set foot out of the estate while you're resting. Is that correct?"

"But, my lady, why are you going to the east?" Sebastian asked.

"First of all, I'd like us to establish the town hall of the port city as a base of operations. I'll leverage my station to do what we can, but before that, I want to confirm the situation with my own eyes. Second, I want to observe the Boltik family for myself—to see what they're all about. Finally, I need to deal with our spoiled little knight. If push comes to shove, I'll approach him myself, but I'd like to resolve the matter without drawing attention. I'll be bringing Dean and Lyle as my escorts. Tanya will join us after she's assigned more spies to watch Van."

"Yes, my lady." Both Dean and Tanya bowed their heads.

"Dean? Go tell Lyle, would you? We'll leave as soon as you're ready."

Accomplishments
of the Duke's Daughter

CHAPTER 16

The Duke's Daughter
Heads into Danger

THUS, WE SET OFF for the east—not in a carriage but on horseback. It was faster that way. Whether because this trip wasn't as grueling as the one to the capital or because I'd grown more used to that mode of transportation, I was in far less rear-related pain by the end of it.

I wore a disguise, of course. The people in town hadn't recognized me when I'd gone incognito there, so I had Tanya do that same makeup on me again. Lyle was disguised this time as well. He wasn't wearing makeup, but he dyed his hair and wore glasses, and he shed his usual armor.

We reached the port city in the east a day later, stopping only to change horses. It was around late afternoon, and the sun hadn't yet set. We could only stay for a week, so we had to act quickly. First, Lyle and I booked a room at an inn, and then I went to observe the town hall. Before I did that, I sent Dean out to gather information in town on a number of specific subjects.

"At a glance, it doesn't seem like anything has changed since our last visit. The only difference is that the mood in the air feels a little heavier, perhaps?" I said.

The town still seemed bright and cheerful, and the people were friendly, just like they had been—but an odd weight was layered over their every action.

"I feel like someone's watching us, and they've got an icy glare... Is it malice?" Lyle murmured, cautiously looking around.

We couldn't do anything with a feeling, so we headed toward the largest building in town, the town hall. There was a reception window as soon as you walked in. The receptionists answered various requests and handled forms, just as they did in any other Armelian town. There were quite a lot of citizens in the hall, and all the staff members seemed busy.

"May I help you?" a woman asked me. She wore a uniform and a name tag, which indicated she was a staff member.

Lyle stepped between us. "I'm thinking of moving to town, and the merchant guild told me that I should check to see what kind of paperwork I'd need to fill out."

"Certainly. Here's a number. Please wait your turn and then bring the number back with you when I call it."

She showed us to a waiting room where we sat down. We'd decided on our story before we came, so we were prepared to stick to it.

"Sorry to keep you waiting," she said when she returned and guided us to her desk. "Please, have a seat."

Lyle answered all the woman's questions according to our

plan, and everything was going smoothly, by the book. He seemed to be making a good impression on the woman.

"Do you have any other questions?" she asked.

"I heard some rumors on the way that things have been less safe here recently. Is that true?"

"Well..." She frowned, seeming reluctant to say. "Honestly... and this is embarrassing, but the rumors are true. In short, some... organizations are competing with each other, and it's impacted the town as a whole."

"I see."

"But don't worry. In Armelia, as you know, we have a garrison of soldiers assigned to each district. They have already been notified, and I'm sure they'll take care of it soon."

"Oh? So you sent a report to the garrison?"

"Yes, quite a while ago. They're in the middle of dealing with another incident and can't come quite yet, but I'm sure they'll be here soon."

"Well, that's reassuring. Thank you."

We left and went straight back to the inn.

"Even a town hall receptionist knows what's going on," Lyle muttered. "She said they'd already notified the local garrison, but do you remember seeing a notice?"

"No, not at all," I said. "And something of this magnitude would've been brought to my attention."

"I haven't heard anything from the garrison either. Something this important definitely should have gone to you before they responded."

"I don't want to doubt our own men, but...I think I'd better go take a look into the local armed forces."

"That's a good idea. Now we need to wait on Dean's report."

At that moment, Tanya entered the room—perfect timing, as usual. "I'm sorry I took so long, my lady."

"I'm glad you're here, Tanya. Is everything all right?"

"Of course."

"Good. Tanya, is it possible to change my appearance even more?"

"I figured you might say that, so I brought a wig from the Azuta Corporation. I can change your makeup as well."

"Wonderful. I'm going undercover at the town hall tomorrow."

"Very well."

Just then, Dean got back, too.

"Well? How was it?" I asked.

"I can't say anything for certain. But...something felt off."

"Off?"

"Yes. There are discrepancies between the accounts we've heard of the Boltik family's activities and the things I've actually witnessed here."

"Did you see something today?"

"Yes. I believe so."

"And? What are they up to?"

"The Boltiks run a company that deals with imports from other countries. It seems they're withholding the products from the general market and only selling them for higher than market value."

"Ah, I see. And if we don't do something about it, the citizens will start to distrust us. Dida heard some citizens theorize that we're trying to steal profits. That might be just what the Boltik family wants them to think."

"Perhaps."

"It's possible they had this planned for a while and started those rumors on purpose—and they took advantage of my excommunication to drive distrust." I sighed. "If Dorssen digs into this, that will only mean more problems for us."

"Yes, let's use Tanya's skills and have her look into this immediately."

"Can you do that, Tanya?"

"Yes, of course."

"Dean, will you come to the town hall with me tomorrow, like we planned?"

"Absolutely."

And so ended our first day in the east.

The next day, Dean and I went to the town hall masquerading as students on the government track of Armelia's academy. We had established a program in the Armelian capital that sent these students out to gain work experience, and we operated under that cover story.

Town halls and other such offices are always short-staffed, and the program gave the students a taste of what their future occupations would be like—especially as there was a good chance most of them would end up working at a town hall.

We introduced ourselves as students who had come to act as interns. I'd already notified the academy of our cover story, just in case someone wanted to do a background check. I felt bad knowing that we were taking away important experience from actual students, so I'd promised the academy that I would do everything I could to get the students who'd originally applied here the positions they wanted.

Putting that aside, I wore a completely different disguise that day. I wore glasses again and a wig that was so black it almost looked blue. Many people had dark hair in eastern Armelia, so I didn't stand out at all. In fact, since this was a port town, there were people of every appearance and hair color that you could imagine.

Dean was also disguised, and the two of us walked through the town hall totally incognito. Our prior arrangements ensured we were welcomed in.

Unfortunately, as students, we couldn't pick the tasks we were assigned to, so Dean and I were separated. There was nothing to be done about that. Actually, I had grown so accustomed to being the one giving out orders that it felt refreshing to receive instructions from someone else.

I delivered documents throughout the building and did simple calculations. None of it was especially complicated, so I finished quickly and had a healthy chunk of spare time on my hands. I enjoyed listening to the staff talk about things I never would have heard during the trip I'd taken to the port as the governor.

"Oh, Alice—you don't have to do that, dear."

"I'd like to learn everything I can while I'm here. Please, allow me." I smiled at the staff member.

I was taking out the trash. It wasn't garbage, though, but documents meant to be burned. This town hall had a rule that papers that had served their purpose were to be burned before the end of the day.

I took the papers out to the charcoal stove—though of course I read every document before burning it.

Bingo, I thought with a smile.

I'd found documents that hadn't actually been properly recorded—statements from citizens, et cetera. These were what I had been after. I'd separated the trash I collected from every individual waste bin, so I knew exactly who had thrown out what. To be precise, I knew who had wanted these documents burned.

I was relieved to have results from the day's work, but even more than that, I found myself glad to have spent invaluable time learning things about the experience that I might not otherwise have been able to.

At the end of the day, I met up with Dean and we exchanged information, then returned to the inn to tell the others.

"Tanya, I want you to look into this person. There's a good chance they're involved in this operation."

"Very well, my lady."

"Yes, thank you. How about you, Dean?"

"I found two others besides the one you indicated. I made a few observations, but I don't think they're directly involved with this matter, so I'll write a report on it later. What made you single out this individual?"

I told him about the documents, and Tanya looked at me with surprise.

"You took out the garbage, my lady?"

"It was my suggestion. I had to—I thought I might be able to find some clues."

"I suppose that's true. This person didn't come up in my investigation. At any rate, I will look into all three people."

"Thank you."

"Of course," she said.

"What about you, Tanya?" I asked. "Did you find out anything today?"

"I did. It seems the Boltik family isn't actually behind this operation. I suppose it would be more accurate to say that they are involved, but they're not the masterminds."

"Why do you think that?"

"Everything I've found about the Boltiks suggests that they wouldn't design an operation like this. It doesn't fit their pattern. I also looked into some people whom Dean said were claiming to be in the family."

"But you found no record of them?"

"Exactly. They belong to a rival gang."

"I see."

"They did communicate with someone who actually belongs to the Boltiks. His name is Emilio, and he's the second in command—so the Boltiks *are* somewhat involved."

"Now the question is whether the Boltik family approved this, or if Emilio went rogue?"

"I think the latter is more likely. Only certain members of the family have shown up in our investigations."

"You're right. Have you found anything regarding Dida?"

"Well…" Tanya hesitated, which was rare for her. I urged her to continue. "I have no idea where he is or what he's doing. I can only surmise, from our last conversation, that he might have been part of the gang whose ringleader is masterminding this operation. In short, he's probably already aware of the information we've been working to gather."

"I see…"

"Shall we mobilize the garrison?" Tanya asked, but I shook my head.

"No, we can't. Lyle's looking into it, but until his report, I can't be sure if they're trustworthy. So if we brought them in…"

"It might only make things worse?"

"Precisely. It's one thing if Dida has been captured, and that's clearly the situation once the authorities intervene. But what if he hasn't been captured because he's infiltrating their operation? Or what if they've caught him, but they're keeping him hostage as insurance? It will still look like he's in on it. If I can't predict how the local soldiers will react…it might be hard for us to cover for him."

"Pardon me for overstepping."

"Not at all. You're right. We need to make a move either way."

"My lady, do you mind if I take my leave for a moment?"

"I wouldn't mind, but what do you intend to do?"

"I'd like to meet up with Lyle. If he has to keep an eye on the garrison, he might not be able to come back soon, and I'd like his report sooner rather than later. He also asked me to let him know if we learned anything important."

I'd thought she was going to ask to do something more closely related to Dida, so I was surprised, but I didn't want to tell her no. "You have my permission."

"I shall take over guarding Lady Iris," Dean said.

Tanya had looked concerned about leaving me, but Dean's words put her mind at ease. As she left, I wondered when she had grown to trust him so much.

"So it's a rival of the Boltik family? Hm..." I murmured. "That means the rumors are true. They're after me...or perhaps they're after Dida."

"I think it's more likely Dida," said Dean. "If they directly targeted you, it would be difficult for them to survive in Armelia, even if they managed to overcome the Boltiks."

"That's true. But the rumors still say it's me they're after... Mmm, I see..."

"I think you're on to something. They probably thought your excommunication was an opportunity. That's why you increased security on Van—because you thought something like this might happen, right?"

I smiled wryly. "I don't know what Emilio was thinking, working with his family's rival, but it seems like he's hiding behind the Boltik name, at least. The import goods they're hoarding are likely hidden at the Boltiks' base. I'm not sure whether the rest of the family would be on my side, though. According to the reports..."

"They probably don't want to publicly antagonize House Armelia. If they knew about the situation, they'd want to get rid of the goods as soon as possible to keep the whole thing under wraps."

"I wish they'd just make a move."

"You don't think they're hesitating *because* of the factional split?"

"Ah, I see what you mean. Their own network is untrustworthy. Some of them may even want it to remain that way."

"Exactly. Their boss made a real mistake this time."

"Dean, would you bring me a map?" I took a deep breath and let it out, trying to calm my nerves. "Ugh. Even if I don't mobilize the garrison, Dorssen might make his move, and that will endanger Dida. It would be very knightly of him—and he takes such pride in his knighthood. Normally, no one would so aggressively poke their nose into the business of another domain, but if anyone would do it, it'd be him."

The knights were meant to protect the royal family first, the capital second. That was the limit of their jurisdiction. So, if the son of an aristocrat serving as a knight interfered with the business of another duchy, it meant trouble for his house. Under normal circumstances, someone in that position would be compelled to abstain from taking action. That was where the Tasmerian military was supposed to come in.

But Dorssen would definitely interfere, especially if he hadn't matured or otherwise changed since my expulsion. He'd act without even thinking of the consequences.

"Here it is." Dean handed me the map. At the same time, I gathered my calm and set aside my feelings. "Dean, you know where the Boltiks' base is, don't you?"

"Why do you say so?"

"Just a hunch. Could you..." I started, but when I saw the look on his face grow tense, I shrugged. "I won't say a thing. You could've learned anything at all in the course of this investigation. Moreover, your family are merchants, and you might very well have interacted with them in that capacity. But no matter the reason, I just...I have a feeling you know their leader. What was it you said—a real mistake this time?"

"Did you..."

"Like I said, it's purely a hunch," I laughed, drawing a tight smile from him.

"Yes, I heard you. I swear I have no true connection to the family, so I don't know much about the structure of the organization."

"You're such a mysterious person," I murmured as I studied him.

"Do you think I can't be trusted? Am I so suspicious?" he asked, glancing at me. It seemed like his eyes were searching for the answer.

"Strangely, I don't believe so. Perhaps that makes me a bad governor." I chuckled.

Dean knelt in front of me as I sat, so he could be at my eye level. We were closer now than before. He leaned in even closer, toward my face. My heart was pounding.

"You are not a bad governor," he said.

"Are you sure?"

"Yes. Please, I want you to use me. I'll let you. I vowed to give you all of myself. Won't I be useful?"

"Ah, yes...that's right. You did say that." I giggled softly at the teasing tone he'd taken on at the end. "Very well, Dean. I want you to help me."

"Of course, my lady. What do you wish me to do?"

"I want to see the boss of the Boltik family. Could we do that now?"

"If we go straight to their headquarters, yes."

"Then take me there. I have to go as soon as possible. I have to save Dida."

"But my lady... You know well that the Boltiks are involved with all number of illicit activities. They're a dangerous group to contact. Are you positive you want to do this?"

"Yes, I do. Dida might be in danger, and Dorssen might be planning to make a move that will seal his fate. Should I hesitate? Should I do nothing?" I couldn't waste this opportunity.

"That sounds like you," Dean said with a soft smile. "Just keep doing what you've been doing, my lady. I will protect you from anyone. So please...entrust your body to me."

That last line got me—I knew he didn't mean it in a romantic way. He was asking me to entrust my body to him for protection, to trust him with my life since we were walking into danger. Yet his words hit me square in the heart, and my mind blanked for a split second.

"Dean..." I whispered. *I want to give all of myself to you. My heart, my body. Everything—except my responsibilities.*

I couldn't say it.

Instead, I smiled. "Yes, Dean. I will."

"Very well, my lady. However..."

"Yes?"

"Let me change into something easier to move around in."

He did so, as did I, and then we met back up downstairs to seek out the Boltik family.

Now that the sun had gone down, a different sort of person was out and about in the town—especially when one happened to be in a back alley.

"This way." Dean pulled my hand, and we made to run.

"Who are you? Argh!"

Dean grabbed the man standing in our way. Dida and Lyle had always made much of Dean's strength, and it turned out that they hadn't been exaggerating.

"What do you want?" the man gasped.

"We want to see Glaus," said Dean.

"What the hell are you talking about? You think Glaus has time to meet with some young punk?"

"That's not for you to decide, is it? And all of you hiding over there—you can come out now."

Several men stepped out from the shadows.

Dean snorted. "What a nice welcoming party. So are you going to let us pass? Or..."

"'Course we can't let you pass!"

Instantly, a fight broke out—but it didn't take long for one side to claim victory. Even though he was vastly outnumbered, the clear winner was Dean.

When he fought, he moved just like Lyle and Dida. He didn't have the stiff, regimented maneuvers of the knights or those in the Armelian guard. I couldn't take my eyes off of him. I suppose you could call it a refined sort of violence. It only took a few moments for him to best every single opponent.

"Are you all right?" he asked me, not even panting.

"Yes. I trust you," I said, clutching his shirt. I meant it, too, from the bottom of my heart. Even so, my hand was trembling. I'd have been lying if I said I wasn't frightened to go where we were going. Dean must have sensed that, because he squeezed my hand. His warmth melted my anxiety away.

"Dean."

"Yes?"

"Have I grown since Dida stopped me from going into that alleyway?"

"Yes. You've grown more vibrant. Both as the governor, and as a woman."

"Smooth as ever. I wonder why hearing it from you gives me so much courage."

"It's all right, my lady. There's nothing for you to worry about.

You can do this." As Dean said that, he rested his forehead on mine. A strange sense of nostalgia washed over me, along with relief. I closed my eyes and squeezed his hand.

That feeling of relief filled my heart.

"Let's go, my lady." Dean said, and we set off again.

Soon, we reached a building that faced the sea. From the outside, it looked like any other building in the neighborhood. Dean hid me in the shadows and dashed toward the entrance. Once he dispatched the man guarding the gate, he returned to me, grabbed my hand, and brought me with him at a run.

Quickly, quietly, we made our way up the stairs. I'd assumed there would be a large number of people inside the headquarters, but there wasn't. I didn't see a single soul. Just as I wondered if we were really in the right place, we reached our destination. Dean paused in front of a door, twisted the knob, and forcefully pushed it open.

At that exact moment, a sword came flying toward us, and I bit my lip to keep from screaming. Simultaneously, Dean blocked the sword with his own and struck it away.

"Stop!"

The second the man fell to the ground with a thud, a deep voice rang out. This room was vast and tall, and the sharp voice echoed within it.

I glanced over and saw several strong-looking men who had frozen in the middle of what they were doing.

"Heh. What a day." Only one man was sitting, and he chuckled throatily.

"Long time no see, Glaus." Dean said with a sigh.

So Dean *did* know him—and pretty well, it seemed.

"Long time no see," said Glaus. Then his friendly attitude abruptly changed. "Looks like you're still causing trouble everywhere you go. Can't you rein it in?"

"That's not very nice. You're talking like I'm always the one making problems."

"Aren't you?"

"Trouble has a way of finding me. I just deal with it. I'm pretty sure you're the one stirring things up lately, in any case."

Glaus's expression tightened a mote. "How much do you know?"

Dean's gaze sharpened just as Glaus's had. "Let's just say I know enough."

"Tell me everything you've got."

"That's rather presumptuous, isn't it?" Dean snorted, and the men near us tensed.

"I said stop!" Glaus growled—to my surprise. He was keeping them in check. "They may not look it, but these guys are real beasts. They're perfectly willing to get maimed or killed if that's what it takes to protect me."

"That's awful. Though I'm pretty sure I could take half of them at once, if it came to it."

That enraged two of the men, and they charged Dean. In no time, he had them flat on the ground. His movements were so fast, I honestly didn't even see what he did.

"Vicious." Glaus laughed. "You never change, Dean. You guys get it now, huh? My bad, my bad. What've you got?"

"I'm not the one who's come to talk to you. It's her."

"A woman?"

They all stared at me.

I took a step forward. "It's a pleasure to meet you. My name is Iris Lana Armelia."

"Armelia…" Glaus smirked. "The daughter of a duke. What are you doing here?"

"I want to make a deal, of course."

Glaus laughed out loud. "Hilarious! A noble maiden, come to make a deal with me? Why don't you run back home to Daddy's mansion, sweetheart? If you leave now, you might make it in time for tea."

"Why, I'd love to. Unfortunately, you've all been such amateurs that I've had to come ensure things get done properly."

Glaus's smile vanished. A dark, intimidating aura rolled off of him. "You'd better watch your tongue. I don't care how noble you are, or if you've got Dean standing in front of you—I don't take kindly to that manner of talk."

I was so frightened that I thought my knees would start knocking together—but I clenched my stomach, maintained my composure, and finally, I smiled. "It seems there's a rumor that House Armelia has joined forces with your family to hoard imported goods and steal profits from the citizens. The people think this quite unfair. Hence why I'd like to resolve the matter as swiftly as possible."

I must have looked out of my mind, smiling in a place like that.

"Of course, it's not a big deal," I went on. "If I act recklessly and die in so doing, all you have to say is that you had nothing to do with the matter from the start. Although, I have a feeling that if the daughter of a noble is murdered, both Armelia's armed forces and the royal army will be mobilized in order to keep the peace. I suspect they'd decide you ought to take full responsibility for the incident. End of story. They wouldn't care who the *actual* mastermind might be. Meanwhile, all I personally care about is taking care of this quickly and keeping my house's name untarnished. Surely you can't object to that, can you?"

Glaus scowled. "Can't lay a hand on you when you put it like that."

"Well, then. I'll get back to the point. I want this matter over and done with. I know you do, too. So, let's work together. That's the deal I want to make."

"I got something to ask."

"Yes?"

"I'm well aware you've got the manpower to crush my family whenever you want. You didn't have to come here all on your lonesome."

"True enough."

"Then why did you?"

"If I destroyed your family, I'd hardly destroy all of your kind," I said. "Moreover, the survivors would grow more cunning. They'd fight dirtier. Thus I've decided that although you're troublesome, I'd rather keep you around. You run this town, do you not?"

Even if the Boltiks' business was illicit, the citizens accepted them. They did in fact control the port. Case in point: I didn't believe the town hall official who had been covering for the Boltik family had been directed to do so by Glaus or his men. Citizens in the dark were concerned, and they wondered what was going on—some more keenly than others. The testimony I'd burned had surprised me, as had the responses from the citizens in town. Numerous individuals suspected that whoever was behind this was impersonating the Boltik family. I now had reason to believe that they were correct.

"Or are you unworthy of their trust?" I asked after I laid all this out. "If so, I'll go ahead and call up my soldiers."

Glaus laughed. The other men did, too. "You got me!" he crowed. "I wondered why you'd bring a girl round here to talk to me, Dean. Now I understand. She's a good woman."

"Isn't she?" Dean said.

My heart skipped a beat.

"I can wrap the truth in all manner of pretty words, but we're rogues, through and through. Even so, we've got our own set of rules—lines you can't cross, no matter what. It would sully our names if we failed to live up to your expectations."

"You'll work with us, then?" I asked. "You'll lend me your power?"

"We will. Although I have a feeling you're going to be the one saving us."

My negotiation was successful. I didn't let it show on my face, but I inwardly breathed a sigh of relief. Now I had a connection with Glaus. It had all been worth it.

But it wasn't over yet. The real battle had just begun.

"Show me the territory under your control."

Glaus nodded. One of the men standing by the wall came over to me with a map. "Here." He pointed out several places.

I studied it and indicated a neighborhood. "Here."

"Why here?"

"The sewers run under that street, and anyone who works with the town officials would have access to it. It would be an excellent location for storing goods, as well as a means of traveling unseen."

"I see."

"And according to Tanya's investigation, their base is right here." I pointed to a specific location in the neighborhood.

Dean seemed impressed. "What are you thinking? Go there now?"

"Soon—first we need to get Tanya."

"All right."

"I've told you where to find them," I said to Glaus. "Now you just need to make your move."

"I hear you," he said. "We'll take care of it. But are you sure this is what you want?"

"Yes. I'd like you at the forefront of this operation. You're more important to the locals than we are. In exchange, all I want is for you to rescue a man with brown hair; his name is Dida. Well, if you think you can pull this off, at least."

"Oho?"

"You can't go into this half-heartedly. If you try to protect your former allies, I won't hesitate to bring in my soldiers."

Glaus chuckled. "Sounds good to me. All right, boys, get ready to move!"

At his call, his men leapt to action, preparing themselves to head out.

"We'll be going, then," I said.

"You do that. But come back and visit when all this is settled! I'd love to have a drink with you."

"Sounds lovely." I nodded. "I'm looking forward to it."

With that, we bid Glaus farewell and made our way back to the main street.

We met up with Tanya immediately after that, and she was incensed. I couldn't blame her. I did ask her to save the lectures for later, because we had places to be.

Tanya also had news—Dorssen was with Dida. As expected, Dorssen had stuck his nose where it didn't belong.

Things had actually turned out rather well for us. It seemed Dorssen had seen a man emerge from the sewers and grown suspicious—at which point he'd gone to investigate the matter himself. He'd stumbled on the true mastermind's base as well as the place where Dida was being held captive.

Dorssen had really gone above and beyond what I'd thought

him capable of. At least if he'd seen Dida being held captive, he had surely realized that we weren't cooperating with the trouble-makers. Luck had been with us in this instance. We might even be able to use Dorssen's testimony to prove our innocence.

To the point, Dorssen had tried to rescue Dida, but he had been ambushed. Now they were roommates.

The one problem with Dorssen's little adventure was that, since he'd discovered the sewer entrance, the gang we were after had sealed it off. We could no longer use it as our point of ingress. We would need another route in order to save Dida. Namely, we'd have to go in through the front.

None of my companions were content to let me stay at the inn alone, so I was going with them—though it was just Dean and Tanya. Lyle had to keep an eye on the local garrison. He'd swiftly identified which of the port town's soldiers had a connec-tion to the gang we were investigating and delivered the proof to Tanya while Dean and I were at the town hall.

Now, while we were making our preparations, Lyle was with the soldiers, going, "Troops! What is the meaning of discipline?" and "You there! What does it mean to be a soldier?" He'd get them all riled up before he led them to our location. In other words, he was buying us time.

It would be a problem if they arrived before the Boltik family was finished, but once they had cleaned house, I would have the soldiers take care of the rest.

Finally, we headed to our destination. The smell of the salty sea air was especially strong by the shore. Our target was one of many large warehouses. We ducked into the shadows just inside the entrance. The Boltik family had just faced off with their rivals in the center of the warehouse, and the groups were shouting at each other.

In the center of it all were Glaus and his treacherous second, Emilio.

"Excuse me for a moment," Dean said as he dashed off into the shadows between the crates. He disappeared into the dark, and I struggled to adjust my eyes to see.

"You really did it this time, Emilio, you bastard!"

"Aw, shut up! You've gone soft, Glaus. I'm the man for the job—not you!"

"You know, you're really showing your own ass, acting like this. Don't worry, though. We'll take on anyone who spits in our faces, even if they're barely worth the trouble. Get 'em, boys!"

At Glaus's signal, ear-splitting war cries rang out. The fight began.

It was a different kind of brawl than I'd ever seen Dida or Lyle participate in, or even Dean. It was brutal.

"What is it, Dean?" Tanya asked when he reappeared beside us.

"The Boltiks figured out a way to get back into the sewers. They're in them now to ensure no stragglers escape."

"They really know what they're doing. Well, my turn."

Tanya moved forward. She slipped around the crowd and in the midst of the chaos, sneaked into the back room. Watching her maneuver around so many hostile individuals without attracting attention—it was really something else.

A tense minute later, Dida emerged from the back room, though he was alone. Even from a distance, I saw that his cheek was red and swollen. If I got any closer, I was sure I'd see even more injuries. Despite his condition, he leapt straight into the fray.

"Wh-what is he doing?!" I gasped, even though I knew he couldn't hear me.

My fear couldn't reach him, so he kept going. Dida soon became the eye of the storm. Everywhere he went, men flew left and right as he flung them aside with pure skill and strength. I was shell-shocked by the display.

Between the Boltiks and Dida, the enemy's ranks rapidly dwindled to nothing.

When Dida stood alone in the center of the warehouse, he sheathed his sword.

"Tory!"

His voice shook as he snarled that name out; I felt it in my own chest. I couldn't believe Dida could sound so grim—but his gaze was deadly serious. I wouldn't have dared make light of it.

A man responded to Dida's snarl, stepping forward.

"That's the mastermind," Dean murmured.

I looked up at him in surprise. Had Dida known who was responsible for this incident from the start?

Meeting Dida face-to-face, Tory balked—but only for a split second. Then he grinned and strode over.

It was obvious even to me that the Boltiks had already won. The enemy had been more or less obliterated, and the only fighting left to do was mere cleanup. But Tory still faced off with Dida.

"You got out already, huh?" he snorted. "Sorry, but you're gonna have to behave for a bit longer. It'll all be over soon anyway. For both of us."

"Let's end this, then." Dida drew his sword again.

I'd never heard such gravity in his tone—and the way he drew his sword made it seem like he was about to perform some kind of sacred ritual.

"You're gonna point that thing at me?"

Dida hesitated for only a moment. "Yes. Doesn't matter what we shared. Not anymore. You moved against my mistress, and for that, you'll get what you deserve."

At Dida's words, Tory burst out laughing wildly. "Oh, now you think you're some kind of knight? You're all high and mighty now, huh? Good for you, being your mistress's pet."

Dida made his move. He had been trained by my grandfather; Tory stood no chance.

In a single lightning-quick movement, Dida struck him with his sword—then as Tory fell, Dida struck him again across the face. Tory didn't even have time to strike back.

The Boltiks had finished off the last of Tory's gang. The only ones left on the field were Dida and Tory. All eyes were on these two men.

"I have one more question for you," Dida said, his voice hoarse. "Why did you do this?"

"Why?" Tory sneered from the floor. "What does it matter?"

"It doesn't. I just wanted to ask before I take you away."

Tory laughed again. "Take me away, huh? Hey. Really, though.

Who d'you think you are, slum rat? You grew up in the same filth as me!"

He screamed that last sentence. It was a pathetic sound.

"Why'd you get so important, huh? Why only you? Why'd you get to walk in the light? You and I—we're the same!"

"Is that what you were thinking?"

"Yeah, it damn well was! I wanted my share of the underworld, sure. But the real reason I did all this was you, Dida!"

Dida's face twisted.

"Why were you the only one who got to go someplace where the sun still shines?" Tory snarled—no. He was sobbing.

"Tory..."

Tory just laughed, as if he were spiting the pain with which Dida said his name. "But now you can go to hell! Go on! Go to hell! What will your precious mistress do when she finds out one of your old buddies was responsible for all this, huh?"

Oh? Did somebody call? I glanced at Dean, and he gave me a wry look, his smile faintly amused.

So I stepped forward. Dean was right on my heels. The Boltiks spotted me as I emerged from the shadows, and they stepped aside to let me pass.

"What will I do?" I asked as I walked into the pale lantern light. "I was thinking I'd tell him to come home with me."

The instant I spoke, both Tory and Dida turned and stared at me in surprise. Was it at my words or my presence?

"I'm Iris—Dida's mistress. It seems you've really taken care of my Dida, hm?" I smiled. As I spoke, the Boltiks began to back up.

I was a bit puzzled, but I kept my gaze on Tory, still on the ground. "I heard your grievances. It seems to me your grudge is rather misplaced."

"What?!"

"I mean, I'm right, aren't I? What reason do you have to resent Dida? Because he made something of himself? Because he devoted himself to brutal, unrelenting training and grew stronger? Or are you frustrated that he's the more skilled between you? Well, it's not like he had any control over that either."

"You bi—oof!" Tory cursed and tried to sit up, but Dida stepped on his chest to pin him down.

"Now if you're mad about the discrepancy in circumstances, even then, your anger is misplaced. If there's anything to resent, it's that I was so powerless that Dida was the only one I could save. Resent *me*. Resent my family. Not Dida."

Both Tory and Dida seemed shocked to hear me say that.

"Although, even if your positions were reversed, I don't believe you'd be much different. You'd still be jealous—just of someone else. Look at all the people you involved in your grudge match, after all. You just want someone to blame for all your insecurities and internal dissatisfactions. You want someone to be the villain for your tragic hero. That's all."

Tory said nothing. He just stared at me, wide-eyed, his expression unchanging.

"Let's pity the man. Let's show some compassion. But I'll not empathize with him."

Tory was like an empty shell, unresponsive.

"Dida. Do you have anything else to say to this man?"

"No, I'm satisfied." Dida smiled. But it wasn't his usual cheerful grin—it hid his hurting heart.

"Bind him, Dean."

I assumed the task would prove too hard for Dida, but he shook his head and took over before Dean could. "It's too late for you," he said to Tory. "There's nothing I can do for you now that you've fallen this far."

We couldn't let Tory go. He had to be arrested and tried accordingly. I shot Dida a look that said, *You understand that, right?* and he nodded.

"You Dida?" Glaus asked as he approached.

"Yeah?"

"I'm Glaus. When I heard you were captured, I figured you had to be a lightweight, but you're really something else. How'd they catch you?"

Dida smiled sheepishly.

Glaus laughed. "You're a hell of a guy. You let your guard down around your old buddy, and he fooled ya, huh? Don't know if I can get behind escorting around a duke's daughter, but I just can't hate idiots like you." He cracked up. "You're a real fighter, too. It's a shame. If she hadn't plucked you out of the slums, I could've had you for myself."

"You can't have him," I retorted.

Glaus laughed even more at that. "I figured you wouldn't let him go. Can't blame me for trying." He looked sideways at Dida. "Seems to me you're more than just lucky. Not that you aren't fortunate. Just keep in mind, Lady Luck is a fickle mistress. If we don't grab the hand that's offered to us, we could lose it forever—but you made the most out of the opportunity you were given. You became such a great man that I'm nearly jealous. Though I'm sure you don't love to hear me say it."

It seemed like Glaus was trying to tell Dida to ignore Tory—that it was more than dumb luck that had made him the man he was.

Dida merely nodded.

I was quite moved by Glaus's speech, to be honest with you. I could tell that he had the kind of charisma that drew such respect from other men that they would follow him without hesitation.

"You've sure got a good eye, Lady. You should give yourself a pat on the back. Now then, mind if we take our share of the loot?"

"That's up to you. I'll be keeping an eye on you regardless."

Glaus laughed again. "All right, we'll be going now. We already tied up Emilio and all our guys who defected with him. Your soldiers will be here soon."

"I'll tell them some concerned citizens settled the situation with the help of the Boltik family. People in town will hail you like true champions of justice."

"Aw, knock it off. I'm not used to that kinda stuff. All right, boys! Let's head out!"

Glaus's men made their way toward the exit. I could tell they were all most pleased with their performance.

"Dida, I need you to go back to your prison."

He frowned. "What?"

"I sent Tanya to tend to you—I wasn't expecting you to come out and take part in all this. I'm sure Tanya knocked out Dorssen so he wouldn't get in the way, but I need you to go join him so the two of you can be rescued by the local soldiers. We can't have word of your connection with the mastermind getting out, and it will help if you're not the only one being saved."

"Very well." Dida hesitated. "My lady, about all this…"

"We can talk later. The soldiers will be here soon."

I knew that whatever Dida wanted to say, it was important—he had just called me "my lady" for the very first time. But time was of the essence.

"I promise I'll hear you out later," I called to him as he made his way back to the back room.

"I'll hold you to that, Princess."

The familiar smirk on his face filled me with relief as I left the building.

Accomplishments of the Duke's Daughter

CHAPTER 17

The Duke's Daughter Speaks on Crimes Committed

Thanks to the port town's garrison, all those responsible for the hoarding operation were arrested. By the time the soldiers arrived, none of the culprits could even stand with how badly they'd been beaten.

According to a concerned female citizen (Tanya), it was the Boltik family who had left them in such a state. The going theory was that the Boltiks had investigated the matter to clear their name and punished the perpetrators accordingly.

It was understood that House Armelia had sent one of the duke's daughter's bodyguards to secretly investigate the incident as well, and he had been rescued by the soldiers of the eastern garrison. This proved that the rumors of House Armelia's collusion with the gangs were entirely baseless.

That was the official report from the garrison, which was now circulating through the town. We still had some loose ends to tie up, but overall, the matter was settled.

It wasn't until three days later that I was able to fulfill my promise to Dida and hear him out. First, he had to give an official statement at the garrison about what had happened to him, and then he had to get his injuries checked out at the hospital.

After all that, he came to see me in my study. The first thing he said to me was: "I'm deeply sorry."

I knew it was rude of me, but my mouth hung open in shock. I mean, this was completely out of character for him.

All jokes aside, I asked, "And what are you sorry about?"

"For everything. If it weren't for me, none of this would've happened. But then I went out east without thinking, got caught, and got you stuck between a rock and a hard place. It was selfish to confront Tory on my own—I mean to say, it was unbecoming behavior of someone in your service, my lady. If you wish to dismiss me, I would not blame you."

I smiled at the effort he was putting into his language. "Dida, the only thing I'd like an apology for is how much you made me worry about you. That's all."

His eyes widened with surprise. "But!"

"You say none of this would have happened if not for you—but Dida, I knew of your past, and I kept you by my side regardless. Without you, I would have only one guard in whom I could place my absolute trust. Without you, I wouldn't be able to walk my streets so freely and without worry. You are essential to how swiftly I've been able to complete my agenda. You said you came here without thinking, but I appreciated your decision to investigate. You knew the lay of the land. The error in judgment was mine—I didn't consider the ramifications of your actions. As for Tory...I chose to step forward and speak in the moment. You absolutely mustn't apologize for that."

Dida grimaced. "But I can't forgive myself."

Once again, his response was so grave. I sighed and smiled at him. "Haven't you already been punished enough, Dida?" I asked him gently. "You trusted Tory. Glaus was right when he guessed how you'd been caught, no?"

Dida looked at me with surprise.

"I know what it feels like to be betrayed by those you trust. I know our circumstances were different, but I understand the sort of wound your heart has taken."

Who had been hurt more terribly between the two of us? I would never dare compare. There was no way to know. I wasn't Dida, and he wasn't me. Neither of us could ever clearly articulate how much our betrayers had meant to us.

I was nevertheless sure that Tory had meant a great deal to Dida. That much had been obvious by the look on his face at the end of their confrontation. I didn't know how deep Dida's pain ran. It very well might have been deeper and greater than any pain I'd ever felt. I couldn't honestly say I knew exactly what he was feeling—but I wanted him to know that he wasn't alone. And if he was suffering that sort of pain, no further punishment could possibly be necessary.

"If you still can't forgive yourself, then dedicate yourself to making it up to me through your work. If you still wish to work for me, of course."

Both the knights and the military had their eye on Dida and Lyle, and now Glaus had tried to recruit him, too. Dida had the skill to take any job he wished.

Dida bowed his head. "I do. I wish to remain in your service, my lady."

"You have my thanks. That means the world to me."

Dida kept his head bowed. It behooved me to continue.

"Dida...I'm so glad you're safe. I needed to hear your cheerful voice again. I kept imagining the worst might have happened. Please, rest today. And tomorrow, I'm looking forward to seeing you back to your old self."

"Yes, my lady." Dida lifted his face and smiled at me, and I sagged with relief.

After Dida left, Tanya entered and placed several reports in front of me. "Has Father Rafsimons responded?" I asked.

"Y-yes. Here it is." She handed me a letter.

"All right. Well, I need to read all this. You're free for the rest of the night, Tanya."

"My lady?"

"You have a number of things you'd like to say to him, don't you? I know how worried you were about Dida."

Tanya frowned deeply. "No, I..." she started to say in a hard voice, but she didn't finish.

I handed her a stack of papers as she stood there, frozen. They were the reports on the eastern garrison that Lyle had prepared for us. She needed to read them before we got back to work.

"I was only teasing," I said. "Can you look over those and then give them to Dida for me?"

"Oh, well, in that case..." Tanya reluctantly took the documents and left the room.

I watched her go and then read the letter from Rafsimons.

"He certainly acts quickly, just as I expected... Now it's time for me to make a move as well," I murmured as I folded the letter and put it away.

"It's me, Dida. I'm coming in." Tanya knocked on the door and opened it.

Dida was sitting in a chair by the window, looking thoughtful. Servants' quarters were typically quite small, but Dida, Lyle, Tanya, and all those serving Iris, including Sebastian, had always enjoyed large rooms for their personal use.

"This report is from Lady Iris. She says to read it before you return to work."

"Thanks." Dida took the papers from her with a smile.

"You should do something about your face before you return as well."

"Did Lady Iris say that, too?"

"Of course not. That's a warning from me."

Dida laughed. Tanya could tell it was forced.

"Just so you know, I haven't forgiven you," she said.

"Harsh. I've already been thoroughly lectured, though."

"Thoroughly? Please! I've barely even started." Tanya scoffed.

She couldn't stop thinking about seeing Dida where he'd been imprisoned. When he'd seen her enter the room, he'd laughed—not in relief, or with delight. It had been scornful. Desperate...

"Are you badly hurt?" Tanya asked.

"Naw, I'm fine. Sorry, but could you get me free?"

"What are you talking about?! I'm here to ensure your safety before the soldiers get here—same goes for the little rich boy over there. We're making sure you aren't used as hostages. And you just want me to untie you? What do you think you're going to do, with all those injuries?"

"Settle things."

"Settle things? Ha! Settle what? Don't make me laugh."

"I'm just doing what I have to."

"What you *have* to do is wait here, with him. If you go out there and Mr. Spoiled here catches sight of you in the fray, he'll link you to the Boltik family and we'll all be in a world of trouble! Or what, are you angling to get captured again? You're too hurt to fight at your usual strength."

"I know my own limits. Those rubes don't stand a chance against me."

Tanya was unmoved. "Bravado. You've been captured once already."

"I let my emotions get in the way of my judgment. I won't make the same mistake twice. I've chucked all that petty sentiment right out the window."

"Then what could you possibly have to settle?"

"I want to end this. If I don't, my ghosts will keep haunting me.

This time, they've endangered the person who means more to me than anything. So I need to go out there and *settle* it, once and for all."

"You can't. Look, what would we even do with him?" Tanya looked down at Dorssen, who lay unconscious on the floor. He was an awfully heavy sleeper if he hadn't woken up by now.

"You're here. If he wakes up, knock him out again."

"But—"

"Please! Otherwise I'll never be able to forgive myself. I could never show my face to Lady Iris, or you, ever again." Dida was, in a word, frantic. "Lady Iris is my mistress. She saved me. I'd lay down my life to protect her. And I'm the reason she's in this mess. I don't expect her to forgive me. If I get caught again or cause any more trouble for her, then I'd rather die than let her get hurt."

"Do you mean that?"

"*Yes.*"

And so, Tanya released Dida from his bonds. He swung his arms about for a bit, testing them, and then stood.

"Even when this is all over," said Tanya quietly, "and you see Lady Iris, and she forgives you...I won't."

"That puts you in the right then, doesn't it?" Dida said, and with that, he rushed out into the fray.

In the present, Tanya opened her eyes. "Do you remember? I won't forgive you."

"I know."

"When I saw you face him, that's when I knew. I knew that he never could've stood a chance against you. That meant you were caught precisely for the reason you cited—you lost to your memories. You turned your back on the things precious to you *now*."

That was what Tanya could not forgive. She wasn't angry with Dida for going to investigate by himself, or even for getting caught. Rather... "Do you truly wish to protect Lady Iris? I thought you were the same as Lyle. But *this* is the truth of you?"

"I don't blame you for thinking that," Dida said with a weak smile.

An answering weakness took over Tanya's heart. She let out a sigh. "So? Is it settled?"

"Yeah."

"Was Tory your ghost?"

"Yeah." Dida sighed deeply. "When I started asking around here in the capital, I realized right away that Tory was involved. So I decided to go see him. Try to get him to stop." Dida spoke so quietly that Tanya had to focus to hear every word.

"And the reason you wouldn't take no for an answer when I tried to tell you to stay behind...was because of your relationship with him?"

"Yeah... He and I, we were like Lyle and me now. Brothers. We were always together. When we scavenged for food, when we played around, even when we joined the gang—we were together."

"Sounds nice. I was alone on the streets."

"Maybe I was lucky in that regard. But look how things ended up." Dida laughed. "One day, the boss ordered both of us to go to another gang's turf. Don't ask why—I don't know. I just had a feeling that it was something dangerous. Like he wanted us to steal something, make trouble. We were just some dirty kids with no protectors. If we were lucky enough to succeed, he'd be happy. If we failed, his rivals wouldn't even peg us for his rats. Whole thing struck me as off, so I told Tory we should make a break for it. But he said, 'If you run from here, where would you go? We don't have anywhere else.' So I went with him, even so."

"And?"

"Went smoothly at first. But halfway in, the other gang caught us. I offered to be the decoy. Told Tory to go ahead and grab the loot and make a run for it. Told him to call for backup. The gang caught me, and they beat the crap outta me, but when they let down their guard, I bolted. And while I was running—that was when Lady Iris found me. You know the rest."

"I'm surprised her father let her take you in. Surely they suspected what you'd been involved in."

"I thought so, too. But Lady Iris was stubborn as ever. And I guess they figured I couldn't do much mischief, what with all the people looking out for her."

"That makes sense."

"And that's how Tory and I parted ways. I was the only one who really escaped. I wish I could've gotten him to come with me, before we ever made that last run. But you saw how it ended up. When I got out there and he told me that he finally wanted out—that he was ready to escape for good...I believed him. But when we met up..."

"He captured you."

"Yup. Looks like I'm no negotiator." Dida laughed, but his face held no hint of a smile. "I probably wouldn't have trusted anyone else in that situation. It was shady as hell. I was a fool to take him at his word. But I wanted to trust him. I thought that was who we were to each other. ...Didn't work. I shouldn't have expected anything. It's just as you said—I lost to my memories."

Dida's fists were balled so tight that his knuckles had turned white. His nails were likely digging into his skin, drawing blood.

"I see..." Tanya let out a sigh and stood. Then she walked over to Dida's desk. The document from Lady Iris was still there. She picked it up again and pushed it into his chest. "Read this. You're coming back to work tomorrow, yes?"

"Y-yeah." Dida was clearly confused by the rapid change in subject.

"You settled the matter, didn't you? And the lady gave you a second chance—so don't blow it. Focus your entire attention on work. No more ghosts to distract you."

"Right," Dida agreed, and his head turned toward the ceiling. But his arm lay across his face; he wasn't actually looking at anything.

"You're hopeless."

"Wanna comfort me?"

"Shan't. How could I ever show my face if I gave in to a man so pathetic?"

"Good point."

Tanya laughed, a bit helplessly. "The thing that connects you and I—and Lyle too—is our desire to protect Lady Iris. As long as we don't waver from that goal, we'll always be headed in the same direction."

Even if they had a difference in opinion or didn't see eye to eye, if their ultimate goal was the same, they would never part ways.

"You'll never waver, will you?" he asked.

"Of course not. I'll protect Lady Iris with my life," she said firmly.

Dida laughed.

"You deviated from this goal in one instance, but in the end, you returned. You settled the matter on your own terms. I suppose I'm relieved. I can't forgive you yet, but I'm confident we can keep on in the same direction."

"I'll have to do my best to stay the course—and to reassure you to the point that you feel comfortable having me at your back again."

"You will."

"Really... This place is so comfortable, I can't stand it... I just can't stand it," Dida murmured, his voice shaking the smallest bit. A tear streaked down his cheek.

Tanya pretended not to see it as she took her leave.

I was somewhat nervous. To be more precise, my body was heavy with the gloom welling within me. The day had come for me to face Dorssen. He had involved himself in Armelia's business. I couldn't just let him off the hook without a word.

More than anything, my concern was with his family. I had to be polite. I couldn't do anything to lower my own house's reputation. So I invited Dorssen to my estate. Of course, Tanya, Lyle, and Dida were with me.

I'd been worried about Dida, but he'd returned to work looking refreshed. Perhaps he'd felt better after talking to Tanya?

I was mulling this over when I received word that Dorssen had arrived. I sat straighter and waited for him to enter the room. A few moments later, there was a knock on the door, and a servant showed him in. He was wearing plainer clothes than usual, likely because he had been traveling. I assessed the look on his face and found that his eyes were peaceful and calm.

"It's been a long time, Dorssen. Please have a seat."

He quietly bowed and did as directed.

"Now what brings you to Armelia?" I asked as Tanya poured us some tea.

"I wanted to learn more about you."

"Oh..." I said, and that was all. That was the last thing I had expected him to say.

"I realized I didn't know a thing about you. All I knew were things I'd heard secondhand before I participated in your humiliation. I realized it was too late, but I started to wonder if I'd done the right thing. Thus I decided to come here and ask your people about you."

"It *is* too late," I said harshly.

No, I needed to listen calmly. Dorssen had asked my people about me because he wanted to learn what sort of person I truly was, had he? But then he would have been relying on secondhand information all over again, just as he realized he had before.

How *had* he concluded that he'd made a mistake? I wasn't

256

looking for some kind of apology from him. Not at all. In fact, it made me uneasy to have him lurking around my domain.

Even though I spoke harshly, Dorssen didn't protest. I would have expected as much from the boy he'd been.

"And what were you planning on doing with the information you gained? You said you were trying to determine whether you had done the right thing. Well, what if you concluded that you had done the wrong thing? What then?"

"I don't know how to answer that."

"This is a waste of my time," I said with a heavy sigh.

"At first, I thought I would apologize to you."

"Oh? So you thought you might have made a mistake, asked around, then decided you hadn't after all?"

"No, that's not it. I thought that I *couldn't* apologize to you. Apologizing wouldn't change the fact that I'd hurt you. It wouldn't let you go back to school. It wouldn't return your fiancé. That's what I concluded."

"Oh, how wonderful for you. True, if you'd come wanting to apologize, I would've turned you away immediately. But let me offer a correction—*you* didn't hurt me. Furthermore, I have no desire to renew my relationship with the prince."

"I hurt you when I restrained you."

"Oh, so you meant *physical* injury. Well, physical or mental, there's nothing you can do to change it," I snapped. "You're right. Your words mean nothing to me, and I want nothing from you. Did you go to eastern Armelia knowing the troubles there? Did you involve yourself on purpose?"

"I wanted to help you."

"Your 'help' is nothing but trouble!" I laughed harshly, and his eyes widened in surprise. "You're a knight. But before that, you're Doruna's only son. What if something had happened to you? How could I ever make it up to your family? People already know that we bear each other long-standing grudges. If some evil befell you in my domain, people would say all manner of things—most likely, that I'd taken my revenge on you."

"Well…"

I let out another sigh. How many times had I sighed since I met him? "You haven't changed a bit. It's wonderful for anyone to have such integrity. But yours is self-righteous. You're so concerned with what *you* think is right that you ignore the needs of the people around you. Then you end up causing trouble because of it, and you don't even take responsibility for your mess. You're like a child dreaming of being a hero."

"I…"

"Am I wrong? The proof is in your lack of conviction when it comes to me. As you said, regardless of whether your action was right or wrong, I'll never return to the academy. Your apology won't undo the damage done to the relationship between Houses Kataberia and Aremlia. The only thing you can do is accept your actions."

Dorssen fell completely silent.

"You're no longer a child who can afford to sit around with his daydreams. In short, if you understand, stay away from me. Stop following me and stalking my lands. Leave Armelia and never come back." I snapped my fan closed. I had a feeling that I was smiling for the first time that day.

"May I ask you one last thing?"

"What?"

"What do you think of the knights?"

"I think they're very proud. They're guardians. But I only know one knight with any degree of familiarity, and sometimes I worry that he traded his pride for arrogance." And that was this knight's cross to bear.

I realized I was basing my opinion of an entire group on one person—but these were my honest beliefs about Dorssen. I wanted to think about him as a person unto himself, but at the same time, I nursed deep suspicions about him.

"I see." For some reason, Dorssen seemed entirely satisfied with that answer. "I'm sorry I took up so much of your time. I'll be going now."

With that, he left.

"Maintain surveillance on him until he leaves Armelia," I ordered Tanya as soon as he was gone. She nodded, bowed, and left the room.

"What do you think?" I asked the two men still standing behind me.

"About him?" Lyle asked. "Well, I can't read his mind..."

I burst out laughing.

"But if a woman my age whose accomplishments far outstripped mine gave me a tongue-lashing like that...I wouldn't be able to sit down and do nothing. It would make me less than a coward."

"Do you think he'll try something again?"

"No. I think he'll grow."

"Grow, will he? I think you're right, Lyle, but...I just can't picture that spoiled little rich boy turning into some kind of man." Dida cracked up.

I had to agree with him. "It seems like you know all too well what Lyle means, Dida."

"Yes. I got quite the earful yesterday."

I didn't ask from whom; I already knew. But I also knew it was why Dida looked so calm now.

I couldn't imagine what would happen with Dorssen, but it didn't matter. I'd said what I needed to, and if he approached me again, I would be merciless. Although I hadn't exactly gone easy on him this time either. I just didn't want to have to deal with him in the first place.

But when it came to a certain other young man...things were different.

"Let's get ready to head out," I said.

Lyle and Dida nodded.

"I'll need both of you with me—as my bodyguards." I smiled. I was more than a little relieved to have them both back at my side, my true guardians.

"You never learn, do you?" I giggled. I was gazing at Van, who was in a prison cell.

"Lady Iris! Please, save me. Someone suddenly grabbed me and put me here! I have no idea what's going on!"

"Do you really think I don't know what you did?" I said, still smiling.

Van's eyes widened with surprise.

You really shouldn't be such an open book, I thought, laughing all the more. "You really were easy to sweet-talk. But thanks to you, I know the names of every last one of the pope's remaining supporters. The church adores me again!"

After I fed the names to Father Rafsimons, he'd moved rather quickly. He owed me a favor because of it. I'd reaped numerous rewards from this harvest.

"How did I give myself away?"

"Do I really have to list your mistakes? You believed them, first of all, and you allowed yourself to become their puppet. Then you used the matter of this imports crisis and tried to manipulate Dorssen to place the blame on me."

The rumors that I was colluding with the Boltik family to steal from my own citizens were grave indeed. If Dorssen had witnessed anything to support the rumors, it would have set off a perfect storm. I'd thankfully chased him out of Armelia before he'd sunk any ships.

Even so, I'd had no active part in this incident. Blaming me for an ongoing problem was a weak argument in theory, but that didn't necessarily matter to someone like Queen Ellia.

Queen Ellia had power and influence; she also had designs on my life. I dreaded to think what would have happened if I hadn't been watching Van and Dorssen—I might not have noticed this vulnerability before the queen took advantage of it.

"I have all the proof, so it's no use inventing explanations. Thanks to your father, your family name means nothing. You're nothing but a regular citizen. The people you were involved with have either been captured or likewise disenfranchised. You have no shield. I am an aristocrat, Van—don't tell me you thought you could plot against me and never suffer the consequences."

"Forgive me! I fell for their words—and they used me!" Van seized the iron bars so hard that they rattled.

My bodyguards stepped in front of me, glowering at him.

"Of course, I've sent a report on this incident to the crown on behalf of Armelia. They'll decide whether you're to be tried under the kingdom's law or under the duchy's. We also need to consult with the church. At any rate, I'm sure your punishment will be quite severe," I said as I turned my back.

Van wailed behind me, but I couldn't understand what he was saying.

"I feel much better now," I said as we left.

"Do you?"

"I thought seeing his face would weaken my resolve."

In my past life, in Japan, I had of course known we had the death penalty for those who committed truly heinous crimes. But it had seemed surreal, like the last resort used in a far-off country. Thus, I had been hesitant to see Van again.

But I hadn't quailed from that brutal likelihood at all. In fact, my thoughts were already drifting back toward my other responsibilities.

"I'm glad, that if it had to be anyone, it was him." I'd handed him a chance to prove me wrong, and he'd smacked my hand away. He didn't even seem honestly remorseful; I'd felt no need to hesitate. "Well, we've done what we came here to do. Let's go."

"Ahh... Looks like we can't use Van or Dorssen anymore." Yuri giggled.

"You never had high hopes for either," Divan noted. "We always said if they actually accomplished anything, it would be by sheer luck."

Yuri nodded in agreement. "You're right. They did all we could have hoped just by stirring up trouble for her."

Their master plan was running smoothly. To Yuri, everything happening in Armelia right now was just a way to kill time. She had fun imagining Iris's panic; that was enough for her.

"You're a terror," said Divan, amused. "Thanks to your tricks, multiple houses have fallen out of favor, and there's a rather amusing merry-go-round of family heads under house arrest."

"Oh, I was being nice. Those people were already whispering so loudly about their loyalty to the pope. They would've fallen sooner or later anyway. I gave them one last chance, but they failed." Yuri shrugged. "They would've caused friction in Queen Ellia's faction anyway, so it isn't like we lost anyone important."

It was Divan's turn to laugh.

"It's a bit unfortunate about Van and Dorssen, though. I thought I'd be able to have more fun with them. I do hate little rich boys." Yuri had been putting together a more elaborate plan for Van, but Iris's spies had been too keen, and she'd had to abandon it. Yuri was put out about it, but she'd at least had a bit of fun.

"That's cruel. I thought you were more like your mother."

"How many times do I have to tell you to stop talking about my mother?"

"Oh, pardon me." Divan smiled. "You should be more grateful, though. She's the reason you grew to be the person you are now."

Yuri laughed coldly. "What is that, some kind of joke?"

"No, just my honest observation. Her example taught you what not to do."

Yuri thought on that for a moment. Divan was right. Her mother had been a prime example of how not to conduct herself.

Yuri's mother had been born in Tweil. She'd come to Tasmeria as a spy, assigned to investigate and send word home. She had infiltrated the royal palace as planned, and at first, things had gone smoothly. But for some fool reason, she had fallen in love with a baron. Yuri wasn't sure why.

Yes, her mother had been very beautiful, and yes, physical appearance could be used as a weapon. But you had to know how to use it wisely. If you were plain, you could blend in with the citizenry. If you were beautiful, you could seduce anyone you liked—the most important people in an enemy country, for example.

Mind you, physical appearance was just one tool.

At any rate, someone as strikingly lovely as Yuri's mother could have used her beauty to seduce whomever she wanted. Why, then, had she *fallen in love* with a baron?

After Yuri was born, Divan had made contact with her mother, though she'd tried to ignore his directives. This scene had been witnessed by a servant of the baron's wife—who had then realized the true identity of Yuri's mother. With that, Divan's plan to have Yuri recognized by the baron and integrated into aristocratic society had become a failure.

The baron's wife sent a threat to Yuri's mother: "You're a stain on the baron's name. You're nothing but trouble. Leave, now— get out of town. If you don't, I'll reveal you to the royal family."

And so, Yuri's mother left. The baron's wife, eager to protect House Neuer's reputation, never said a thing.

Yuri didn't understand why her mother had so easily abandoned her plan. She could have blackmailed House Neuer, simple as anything. The house would have been dishonored if the baron's indiscretion with her mother had come to light. Instead, her mother up and left, so as not to cause him trouble. She didn't even make preparations for her departure—she fled with nothing but the clothes on her back. She managed to safely give birth to Yuri, but they had no money, and life was terribly hard.

On top of that, when a pregnant woman was on her own with nothing to her name, people were given to speculate. Even as a child, Yuri picked up on this. People said and did many cruel things to her. It started small—exclusion and the like. Then it escalated to verbal harassment and insults. When Yuri asked her mother why she didn't have a father, she received no answer.

If Divan hadn't found Yuri one day and told her the truth, she likely never would have known.

Divan had taught her a lot of things. He taught her how to observe people and how to speak to them in a way that would win their favor. He taught her that the world was big, much bigger than the small world she was confined to, where everyone was cruel to her.

Yuri kept the fact that she had met Divan a secret from her mother. She felt a bit guilty for keeping a secret, but at the same time, it was thrilling.

Then, soon after she first met Divan, her mother collapsed from a sudden illness. It might have been cured with a certain medicine, but that medicine was horribly expensive, and Yuri couldn't afford it.

Divan had been away at the time—some manner of business. Yuri had been unable to go to him for help. So, she had gone to see the baron whom Divan had told her so much about. She hoped that maybe he would help. She didn't even get the chance to ask; she was turned away at the gate. Worse, the baron's wife, who had already threatened to kill Yuri's mother, came after the girl herself.

Luckily, Divan saved her in the nick of time. Who knew what would've happened to her if not for him?

He gave her a good scolding afterward. If she'd only put some thought into her actions, he said, she would have realized showing her face would anger the baron's wife—not to mention the trouble it could have caused for Tweil.

"But the baron is my father, isn't he?! I'm sure he'd help me if he knew what was going on!" Yuri screamed.

But Divan chastised her. "Stop dreaming," he said.

It didn't matter if the baron had truly loved her mother. He wouldn't divorce his wife. After Yuri's mother disappeared, he hadn't even searched for her. He hadn't cared.

Yuri didn't argue. In fact, she accepted Divan's words as truth.

When it came down to it, she realized, relationships were all about deception. The person who could outmaneuver the other was the winner. Divan had taught her that. Love was the same as all the rest. Whoever truly fell in love first lost. Whoever believed love was real lost.

So her mother had lost. It was so simple, so obvious. Therefore, Yuri would fight, and she would get the best of everyone else. The townspeople who looked down on her, the baron and his family—even her mother, who had trapped her in this situation in the first place.

Outsmart, get revenge, stand on top of all those who'd stood on her. Yuri vowed to do just that.

She lost her first battle, however. Yuri's mother died before Yuri could overcome her. Divan had acquired that expensive medicine she needed, but it was too late.

Strangely, Yuri didn't cry. All she felt was pity. Her poor, pathetic mother. When you lost, the only thing waiting for you was a miserable death. So Yuri would never become like her mother. She wouldn't be able to show her mother true triumph, but she could use her mother's past choices to her benefit.

Yuri had no attachment to Tasmeria. No one there had ever helped her. They were nothing but her enemies, and the kingdom had been nothing more than her prison. She didn't care what happened to it. Instead, she would succeed her mother—and she would be even better.

"You were right. As soon as the baron's wife died, he took me in right away. That man became quite a good teacher. It was so amusing, I had to laugh."

Yuri lived among the aristocracy now. She had nurtured relationships with the nobility before making her official debut into society. Most importantly, it had become her hunting grounds for a potential husband.

In the name of that hunt, she had exhaustively studied etiquette before she entered the academy. She knew better than to just learn the bare minimum required to attend.

When she arrived, she had to admit that it was a bit refreshing to see other people using their family members as pawns as well.

Her father had wanted her to use his family's connections to make friends, but she'd laughed off the idea. What, go straight from the streets to charming high society? Please. She was far more realistic than that.

But she knew how to use what he had correctly, and to her true advantage. The lessons she'd learned from Divan were, in the end, far more useful than the ones she took from the baron.

"Well, none of that matters, in any case. Divan, isn't it about your time to shine? Do please entertain me."

"Of course," Divan replied with a grin.

Seeing the smile on his face brought a smile to Yuri's face as well.

Accomplishments *of the* Duke's Daughter

Afterword

THE THIRD VOLUME. I can't believe we're at the third volume! Not only that, the first volume of the manga was released at the same time. That installment has a lot of characters, so there are a ton of dresses and jewelry. It must've been a lot of work to draw! Since I'm not great at art, I can't even imagine. I'm so glad I get to read the story of the duke's daughter as told by Suki Umemiya's beautiful work.

I had to ask for a lot of favors from my editor this time around. I wrote so much that I wasn't sure if it would all fit in one volume. But if it had to be split up, the first volume would've ended on quite the cliffhanger! It all started when I told her I couldn't cut down anymore scenes. Once she gave me the okay on that, I started thinking about scenes I wanted to add...and I just got even more demanding! She was a brand-new editor for me, too, so I'm really sorry for all that!

Thanks to her, I was able to present my readers with a substantial story, and I'm glad it turned out the way I envisioned it.

Finally, I'd just like to thank all of you. I've only come this far because of my readers and everyone who has supported me. Thank you so much.

—REIA

Let your imagination take flight with Seven Seas' light novel imprint: Airship

A Tale of the Secret Saint

NOVEL 1

Touya
illustrated by chibi

NOVEL 1

She Professed Herself Pupil of the Wise Man

Written by Ryusen Hirotsugu

Illustrated by fuzichoco

Monster Musume
Monster Girls on the Job!

novel by YOSHINO ORIGUCHI

art & character design by OKAYADO

THE HAUNTED BOOKSTORE
Gateway to a Parallel Universe
1

By Shinobumaru

NOVEL 1

Written by Shoji Goji
illustrated by Booota

LONER LIFE
IN ANOTHER WORLD

NOVEL 1

I Swear I Won't Bother You AGAIN!

WRITTEN BY Reina Soratani

ILLUSTRATION BY Haru Harukawa

Discover your next great read at
www.airshipnovels.com

Airship

Experience all that SEVEN SEAS has to offer!

Happy Kanako's Killer Life

STORY & ART BY TOSHIYA WAKABAYASHI

1

HELLO WORLD
THE MANGA

MANGA BY MANATSU SUZUKI and YOSHINORI SONO

I GOT CAUGHT UP IN A HERO SUMMONS, BUT THE OTHER WORLD WAS AT PEACE!

STORY BY Toudai
ART BY Jiro Heian

MANGA 01

Bloom into You
ANTHOLOGY
Volume One

Skip and Loafer

story and art by MISAKI TAKAMATSU

volume 1

STORY & ART BY Eri Ejima

Young Ladies Don't Play Fighting Games 1

Life of Melody

Mari Costa

01
Volume One

My Wife Has No Emotion

Story & Art by Jiro Sugiura

The Masterful Cat is Depressed Again, Today

1

Story and Art by Hitsuzi Yamada

SEVENSEASENTERTAINMENT.COM
Visit and follow us on Twitter at twitter.com/gomanga/

Seven Seas